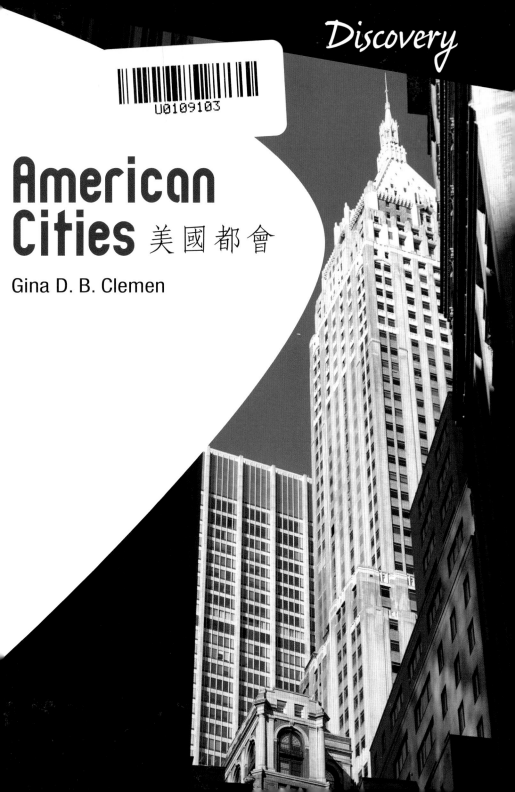

Discovery

American Cities 美國都會

Gina D. B. Clemen

U0109103

Editor: Rebecca Raynes
Design and art direction: Nadia Maestri
Computer graphics: Maura Santini
Picture research: Laura Lagomarsino

Picture credits
Cideb Archive; De Agostini Picture Library: 11, 22, 31, 69, 86 left; © Fine Art Photographic
Library / CORBIS: 17; © Geoffrey Clements / CORBIS: 19; © Bettmann / CORBIS: 21, 43,
53, 55, 60, 62, 77 top, 86, 95; © Jose Fuste Raga / Corbis: 29; © Alan Copson / JAI / Corbis:
30; Library of Congress, Prints and Photographs Division Washington, DC: 41, 57, 61, 83
top; © A.J. Sisco / Corbis : 52 bottom; © Allen Ginsberg / CORBIS: 63; Getty Images: 71;
© Gerald French / CORBIS: 73 top; © Thierry Orban / CORBIS: 78 top; ullstein bild –
Granger Collection: 83; © PoodlesRock / CORBIS: 84; PARAMOUNT PICTURES / Album:
93, 96; HOLLYWOOD PICTURES / Album 94; AFP/ Getty Images: 104.

書　　名：*American Cities* 美國都會
作　　者：Gina D. B. Clemen
責任編輯：黃家麗　王朴真
封面設計：張毅
出　　版：商務印書館(香港)有限公司
　　　　　香港筲箕灣耀興道3號東滙廣場8樓
　　　　　http://www.commercialpress.com.hk
發　　行：香港聯合書刊物流有限公司
　　　　　香港新界大埔汀麗路36號中華商務印刷大廈3字樓
印　　刷：中華商務彩色印刷有限公司
　　　　　香港新界大埔汀麗路36號中華商務印刷大廈14字樓
版　　次：2013年6月第1版第1次印刷
　　　　　© 2013 商務印書館(香港)有限公司
　　　　　ISBN 978 962 07 1999 8
　　　　　Printed in Hong Kong

Contents

The text is recorded in full.

These symbols indicate the beginning and end of the passages
linked to the listening activities. 標誌表示與聽力練習有關的錄音片段開始和結束。

Before you read

1 Text your knowledge
How much do you know about America? Take this quiz and find out!
Choose the correct answer — A, B or C.

1   How many states are there in the United States of America?
  A 52   **B** 50   **C** 48

2   Which is the biggest American state?
  A Texas   **B** California   **C** Alaska

3   Who was the first American president?
  A George Washington   **B** Abraham Lincoln   **C** Thomas Jefferson

4   Where was gold discovered in 1848?
  A San Francisco   **B** New York   **C** Sutter's Fort

5   When do Americans celebrate Independence Day?
  A July first   **B** July fourth   **C** Thanksgiving

2 American and British English
Do you know how American English and British English words are
used? Match the following. You can use a dictionary to help you.

American English		British English	
1	sidewalk	**A**	present
2	railroad	**B**	motorway
3	apartment	**C**	railway
4	gift	**D**	flat
5	subway	**E**	shop
6	store	**F**	pavement
7	billboard	**G**	underground
8	freeway	**H**	lift
9	elevator	**I**	jewellery
10	jewelry	**J**	hoarding

3 Vocabulary

Which jobs do these people do? Match the words in the box below with the definitions. You can use a dictionary to help you.

cattlemen traders hunters outlaws farmers shopkeepers

1   They buy, sell and exchange things. ....
2   They do not respect the law. ....
3   They manage farms. ....
4   They kill animals for food or sport. ....
5   They work in a shop. ....
6   They look after cows and bulls. ....

4 Match the following words with their description.

1   ☐ pioneers   7   ☐ horizontally
2   ☐ timber   8   ☐ colony; colonial
3   ☐ trading posts   9   ☐ Founding Fathers
4   ☐ settle   10   ☐ vertically
5   ☐ fur   11   ☐ Protestant
6   ☐ Pilgrims and Puritans

A   Go to a new place to live and work.
B   Wood that is used for building.
C   A country or area under the control of a distant country; related to that country or area.
D   Part of the Christian Church that separated from the Roman Catholic Church in the 16th century.
E   Two groups of people who were part of a Protestant religious group.
F   Places where goods were bought, sold or exchanged.
G   The first people to explore and live in an unknown area or country.
H   In a flat or level way.
I   In an upwards direction.
J   The soft hair on an animal's body.
K   They were the first people who set up the American colonies.

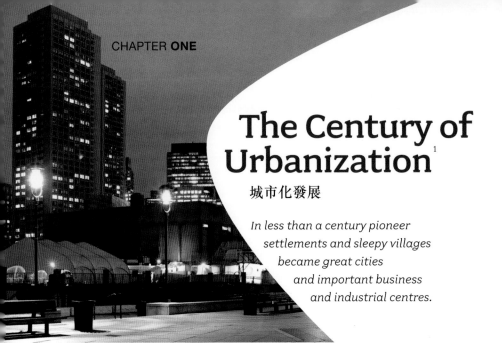

CHAPTER ONE

The Century of Urbanization[1]

城市化發展

In less than a century pioneer
settlements and sleepy villages
became great cities
and important business
and industrial centres.

The United States, not including Hawaii and Alaska, covers about 3 million miles^2, or almost 8 million km^2. It is about the same size as the whole of Europe.

At the beginning of the nineteenth century most of America was a wilderness [2] and no American had ever travelled across the continent to the Pacific Ocean. At the end of the same century there were already forty-five of the present fifty states.

The late nineteenth century was called "the age of great cities" because between 1860 and 1910 the American urban [3] population had grown from six million to forty-four million. By 1920 more than half of the population lived and worked in urban areas. The great speed with which America was settled and its

1. **urbanization** : 城市化
2. **wilderness** : 荒野
3. **urban** : 城鎮

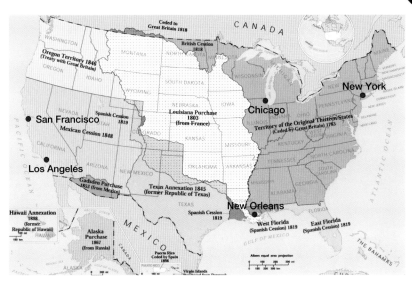

United States map depicting territorial acquisitions.

cities were created is amazing. How did all of this happen? In order to understand the fast growth and urbanization of America it is important to go back to the Founding Fathers.

The North Atlantic Coast

The first attempt at a colonial city in the New World was the British colony of Jamestown in Virginia in 1607, which failed. Between 1620 and 1630 the Pilgrims and Puritans, often called the Founding Fathers, left Great Britain and settled on the northeast coast of North America in the area that is now Boston in Massachusetts. Both the Pilgrims and Puritans were part of a Protestant religious group and went to the New World to practice their religion freely. Their strict religious opinions influenced every part of their life: social, political and economic. They were honest, thrifty [1] and believed in hard work and a good

1. **thrifty** : 節約

The Pilgrim Fathers Boarding the "Mayflower", color print after a painting (end of 19th century) by Bernard Gribble.

education for everyone. Success at work and making money were considered a sign of God's favour. This became known as the American work ethic [1] and it strongly influenced the future growth of the nation.

Soon after their arrival in the New World the Founding Fathers set up the first British colonies and started successful businesses: the fish, fur, salt and timber trades. Businesses and factories quickly developed in and around Boston, which soon became an important city and seaport.

The work ethic of the Founding Fathers soon moved to the rest of New England and the North Atlantic Coast, where trading posts and businesses were set up, grew and became cities like New York, Philadelphia and Pittsburgh.

At this time the life and economy of the South Atlantic area were agricultural. Towards the end of the 1800s the South became more industrial, in particular Texas with its cotton, cattle [2] and oil industries.

1. **ethic** : 倫理
2. **cattle** : 牛

The Midwest

After the American Revolution (1775-1781) the thirteen British colonies became the first thirteen states of America, and their inhabitants [1] were ready to explore and settle the unknown continent.

The first pioneers crossed the Appalachian Mountains and settled in what is now Kentucky, Tennessee, Ohio, Illinois and Indiana, all the way to the Mississippi River, the western limit of America at the end of the 1700s.

In 1803 Fort Dearborn, a U.S. military fort, was built where the city of Chicago stands today. The location on Lake Michigan, the building of the Erie Canal, which connected Lake Erie in the Midwest to New York, and the excellent railroad connections attracted thousands of settlers to Chicago, which became an important industrial city of the Midwest.

Other Midwest cities that grew in size and importance in the 1800s were Cleveland, Detroit and Milwaukee.

The Louisiana Purchase

In 1803 the American President Thomas Jefferson bought an enormous piece of land from France for $15 million: this was called the "Louisiana Purchase". No one knew exactly how big the land was so President Jefferson asked Meriwether Lewis and William Clark to explore it and bring back detailed maps and other information.

1. **inhabitants**：居民

The journey of about 50 men, which began in St Louis, Missouri in 1804, traveled up the Missouri River, crossed the Rocky Mountains, and after many difficulties arrived at the Pacific Ocean in November 1805. They returned to Missouri in September 1806 with maps of the new area of land and very useful information. The Louisiana Purchase doubled the size of the United States and opened the doors to the West.

This was the beginning of the continental growth; hundreds of thousands of people moving from the Atlantic coast and the Midwest started looking for better economic opportunities in the enormous new area of land.

Manifest Destiny

"Manifest Destiny" was the idea that the future of the United States was to grow from the Atlantic to the Pacific, taking its culture, language and government across the continent, while building towns and cities where Americans could live, work and grow rich. The term "Manifest Destiny" means that the idea was obvious — "manifest", and certain — "destiny". It was first used in the 1840s by the journalist John O'Sullivan, but the project for continental growth was first mentioned by Benjamin Franklin in 1767 and by John Quincy Adams in 1811.

American Progress by John Gast (circa 1872), is an allegorical representation of Manifest Destiny. Here Columbia, the female personification of the United States, leads American settlers to the West.

Railroad workers celebrate the completion of the first Transcontinental Railroad on May 10, 1869.

"Manifest Destiny" also meant taking the continent away from the original inhabitants, the American Indians, who fought bravely against the U.S. army and the settlers. By the end of the nineteenth century the American Indians had lost their homes and way of life forever, and were sent to live on reservations [1].

The movement towards the West began in the spring of 1841 in the frontier town of Independence, Missouri, where pioneers and covered wagons [2] met and began their long journey. Who were the pioneers? They were brave, hardworking farmers, hunters, traders, cattlemen, shopkeepers and there were outlaws, too. The American government often gave them free land to settle. They crossed the Great Plains and some settled there, founding towns like St Louis, Des Moines, Omaha and Kansas City, which later became important cities.

1. **reservations** : 保留區

2. **a covered wagon** :

Other pioneers stopped at the Rocky Mountains and founded the cities of Denver and Salt Lake City. Others followed the Oregon Trail, which brought them to the North Pacific Coast, where settlements like Seattle and Portland were founded.

The pioneers who travelled on the California and Santa Fe Trails arrived in California, which was part of Mexico until 1848, and settled in the Spanish towns of San Francisco and Los Angeles. The California Gold Rush and the Transcontinental Railroad made the growth of cities in the West possible.

The Urban Revolution [1]

During the second half of the nineteenth century the United States experienced a great urban revolution and a huge wave of immigration from other countries. As factories and industries grew, cities quickly expanded both horizontally and vertically to make room for their huge populations. New methods of transportation [2] such as the streetcar [3], the subway system and later the car were important for the horizontal growth of cities. Cast-iron, steel frames [4] and the elevator made vertical growth possible.

The cities you will read about were chosen because their history, architecture, culture, geographic location and people are special.

1. **revolution** : 革命
2. **transportation** : 運輸
3. **a streetcar** : 電車
4. **cast-iron, steel frames**: 鑄鐵，鋼框架

The text and **beyond**

PET **1** Comprehension check

Read these sentences about Chapter One. Decide if each sentence is correct or incorrect. If it is correct, mark A. If it is not correct, mark B.

		T	F
1	By 1920 there were fifty states in America.	☐	☐
2	The Pilgrims and the Puritans, also called the Founding Fathers, worked in the fish and salt industries in Massachusetts.	☐	☐
3	Their religious ideas became known as the American work ethic.	☐	☐
4	The people of the South Atlantic area were influenced by the ideas of the Founding Fathers.	☐	☐
5	The pioneers fought the American Revolution in the Appalachian Mountains.	☐	☐
6	Fort Dearborn was built on Lake Michigan.	☐	☐
7	American continental growth started with the Louisiana Purchase.	☐	☐
8	Benjamin Franklin was against the idea of Manifest Destiny.	☐	☐
9	Every pioneer family was given free land to settle in the Great Plains.	☐	☐
10	New kinds of transportation made horizontal growth in cities possible.	☐	☐

2 Vocabulary

Circle the word that doesn't belong and explain why.

0   streetcar (ship) railroad   subway system

A ship travels on water, the other three involve travel on the ground or under the ground.

1   business   industry   factory   government
2   thrifty   honesty   wealth   education
3   inhabitant   pioneer   journalist   settler
4   city   town   state   village
5   coast   trail   path   road

PET ❸ Sentence transformation

For each question complete the second sentence so that it means the same as the first. Use no more than three words.

0   Lewis and Clark built Fort Clatsop on the Pacific coast.
Fort Clatsop was built by Lewis and Clark on the Pacific coast.

1   Traveling across the Rocky Mountains during the winter was not easy.
It .... to travel across the Rocky Mountains during the winter.

2   William Clark was an exceptional scientist.
William Clark was very .... science.

3   President Thomas Jefferson was very popular in the 1800s.
Everyone .... President Thomas Jefferson in the 1800s.

4   The little settlement on the lake was called Chicago.
The .... little settlement on the lake was Chicago.

❹ History

President Thomas Jefferson made the Louisiana Purchase in 1803. What do you know about this time? Answer these questions with a partner. You can use the Internet or an encyclopedia to help you. Decide if the following events happened before or after 1803.

		Before	After
1	The French Revolution begins.	☐	☐
2	The printing press is invented.	☐	☐
3	Gold is discovered in California.	☐	☐
4	Ludwig van Beethoven is born.	☐	☐
5	The American Civil War begins.	☐	☐
6	The first modern steam engine is invented.	☐	☐
7	The Panama Canal is built.	☐	☐
8	Sir Francis Drake circumnavigates the world.	☐	☐
9	Alexander Graham Bell invents the telephone.	☐	☐

Class Discussion

What was happening in your country at this time? Make a list of some important events that happened in your country during the early 1800s and discuss them with a partner.

Before you read

1 Quiz

How much do you know about New York City? Read the questions and choose an answer — A, B or C.

1   Where is the world's biggest public Halloween parade?

   A ☐   Times Square
   B ☐   Fifth Avenue
   C ☐   Greenwich Village

2   Which is the world's largest department store, with over 500,000 different products?

   A ☐   Rockefeller Center
   B ☐   Macy's
   C ☐   Bloomingdale's

3   How did Wall Street get its name?

   A ☐   It is an abbreviation for Wallace-Moore Street.
   B ☐   "Wall" was the last name of a famous New Yorker.
   C ☐   There was a wall there in the late 1600s.

4   Why did hundreds of pigs walk down Wall Street in the early 1800s?

   A ☐   They wanted to eat the garbage.
   B ☐   The area was a pig farm.
   C ☐   The city's biggest butcher shop was on Wall Street.

5   Why are cabs in the city yellow?

   A ☐   All cabs in America are yellow.
   B ☐   John Hertz, the cab company's founder, decided that yellow was the easiest color to see.
   C ☐   Yellow is the color of New York's state flag.

6   What is beneath the Federal Reserve Bank on Wall Street?

   A ☐   The city's biggest subway station.
   B ☐   The computer center for all New York City banks.
   C ☐   Twenty-five percent of the world's gold bullion.

Check your answers on page 111.

CHAPTER TWO

New York City— The Beginnings

紐約崛起

*Originally a Dutch possession,
then a British colony,
New York City was America's
capital for five years
and became the nation's
largest city.*

The Population Explosion

In 1614 the Dutch set up a fur trading settlement on the southern tip of Manhattan Island and called it New Amsterdam.

Peter Minuit of the Dutch West Indies Company bought Manhattan Island, which today is part of New York City, from the Lenape, a native American people, in 1626. He paid them with cheap jewellery and other small objects. Today Manhattan is one of the most expensive places to live.

New Amsterdam became a British colony in 1664 and its name was changed to New York, after the English Duke of York and Albany. New York City quickly grew in importance as a trading port and became the second biggest city of the British colonies with about 20,000 inhabitants.

During the American Revolution many important battles were fought in and around New York City, particularly on Long Island, Staten Island and Manhattan. After the American Revolution New

York became an independent state and New York City became the nation's capital from 1785 to 1790, where George Washington was elected first President of the United States. By 1790 the city became the largest in the United States and it still is today, with about 8,275,000 inhabitants.

Transportation

New York City's economic, industrial and population growth in the nineteenth century was amazing. There were many causes for the city's change. Transportation was one of these causes; its huge natural harbor was full of sailing ships and steamships which imported and exported all kinds of goods. Today a walk or bike ride along the 32-mile Manhattan Waterfront Greenway gives you an idea of the size and importance of this harbor.

The opening of the Erie Canal in 1825 brought more wealth to the city. The Erie Canal connected the Hudson River in New York with Lake Erie in the Midwest. Barges [1] travelled along the canal transporting goods from New York City up the Hudson River to Albany, and then onto the Erie Canal all the way to Lake Erie.

1. **barges** : 駁船

Shipping near the Statue of Liberty (1897) by Christian Cornelius Dommerson.

With this canal the Great Lakes region and the Midwest became huge markets for New York City's products, and the city's economy grew. With the first railroads in the 1830s products from the East Coast traveled even further West.

All kinds of industries — factories, businesses, offices and shops opened in the southern part of Manhattan and several businessmen, like John Jacob Astor, became millionaires. The rich families moved to Upper Manhattan and built magnificent mansions [1] along Fifth Avenue, which can still be admired today. The first brownstone [2] homes, typical of New York City today, were built in the early 1800s for the upper-class families. They are all very similar, with stairs that lead to the front door on the first floor and with servants' rooms at or below street level. The Dakota was the first luxury apartment building built in Manhattan's Upper West Side, across the street from Central Park. You can see the date of when it was built on the front of the building: 1881. Through the years movie stars and famous people have lived here, like singer and composer John Lennon.

1. **mansions** : 豪宅
2. **brownstone** : 赤褐色沙石

The Dakota Apartment House in Central Park West, New York City.

Immigration

Another important cause of New York City's amazing growth and economic success was immigration. At the start of the nineteenth century the city's population was about 60,000. There was a lot of land and jobs in America and this attracted European immigrants from northern and western Europe who were looking for better economic opportunities and political and religious freedom.

Thousands of European immigrants entered the United States through the busy port of New York and most of them decided to live there because they did not have enough money to travel any further. They quickly found a home and started working in one of the many industries and businesses that needed workers. Immigrants were usually poor and went to live in the Lower East Side of Manhattan in crowded, unhealthy apartments called tenements, which often had no windows, heating or bathrooms.

Today the Lower East Side has kept its ethnic [1] character with colourful neighbourhoods like Chinatown, Little Italy, and part of the Jewish community [2]. You can visit the Lower East Side

1. **ethnic** : 種族
2. **community** : 社群

Five Points (1840) a slum area of Manhattan from 1820 to 1890.

Bagpipers[1] marching up Fifth Avenue in the Saint Patrick's Day Parade, NYC.

Tenement Museum at 90 Orchard Street and see how the first immigrants lived.

By 1860 New York City's population increased to about 800,000. The Irish made up the largest group of immigrants, followed by the Germans and the British. The Irish population of New York City has always been proud of its history and as early as 1762 started the traditional St Patrick's Day Parade [2] on March 17. It is the biggest St Patrick's Day parade in the world, and it is great fun to watch from the steps of the Metropolitan Museum of Art on Fifth Avenue, from where you get the best view. On St Patrick's Day New Yorkers wear something green in honour of the Irish, so remember that when you go to the parade!

After the American Civil War (1861-1865) many African Americans from the southern states went to the industrial north, and by 1916 New York City had the largest African-American population in the nation.

1. **bagpipers** : 風笛手
2. **a parade** : 遊行

Ellis Island

In the 1870s a lot of immigrants started coming from southern and eastern Europe and Russia. For years immigrants had passed through Castle Garden Reception Centre of the Port of New York until it closed in 1890. A new centre opened in 1892 on a small island south of Manhattan, Ellis Island Immigration Station. Here government officers checked the immigrants' documents and doctors gave them a quick physical examination before allowing them to enter the country. Between 1892 and 1954 about twelve million people who believed in the American dream [1] passed through here.

Ellis Island is near the Statue of Liberty, on Liberty Island, which was a gift from the French government in 1886. The Statue of Liberty became a symbol of

1. **American dream** : 美國夢
2. **skyline** : 天際線
3. **a dock** : 碼頭

An immigrant family looking at the New York City skyline [2] on the dock [3] at Ellis Island (1925).

hope and freedom for the immigrants who sailed near it on their way to Ellis Island. Today thousands of tourists take the ferry boat to Liberty and Ellis Islands and visit the statue and the Ellis Island Museum.

Several nineteenth-century immigrants made a large amount of money in New York City. Irish-born Alexander T. Stewart became the owner of America's largest department store on Broadway and one of the richest men in New York City. Victor Herbert, another immigrant, became one of America's most famous composers of operettas [1]. Fiorello La Guardia, who was the son of Italian immigrants, became one of New York's greatest and most-loved mayors [2] between 1934 and 1945.

The 1920s

The 1920s were good years for the economy all over the United States and in particular in New York. There were jobs for everyone, the economy was doing well and people were happy. This period was called "The Roaring Twenties".

One of America's best magazines, *The New Yorker*, was first published in 1925 in Manhattan. Some of the world's most famous writers have written for this magazine.

On May 20, 1927 the American pilot Charles Lindbergh began his non-stop flight across the Atlantic Ocean at Roosevelt Field in New York. His flight to Paris took him thirty-three and a half hours and the whole world talked about it. When Lindbergh returned to New York City in June there was

---

1. **operettas** : 輕歌劇
2. **mayors** : 市長

a huge parade in his honour and more than four million people were present. Celebrations lasted an entire day.

Wall Street on lower Manhattan Island became an important financial centre at the start of the nineteenth century. The New York Stock Exchange (NYSE) was the biggest stock market in the world. The Wall Street Crash of 1929 was the worst stock market crash in the history of the United States. Millions of people lost all of their money in a few days. The period that followed was called The Great Depression, because most Americans had lost their jobs and had become poor. The Wall Street Crash influenced the economies of the world, and the depression lasted over ten years.

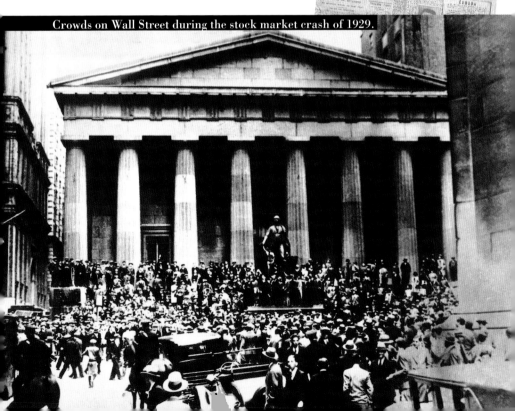

Crowds on Wall Street during the stock market crash of 1929.

The text and **beyond**

PET ① Comprehension check

For each question choose the correct answer — A, B, C or D.

1 The Lenape people sold Manhattan Island to
   A ☐ George Washington.
   B ☐ Peter Minuit.
   C ☐ the Duke of York and Albany.
   D ☐ Holland.

2 New York City's population and economy expanded
   A ☐ and it became the nation's capital.
   B ☐ because millionaires like John Jacob Astor lived there.
   C ☐ because the NYSE opened.
   D ☐ because the Erie Canal was built.

3 Ever since 1881 important people have lived
   A ☐ in South Manhattan.
   B ☐ in the Brownstone houses.
   C ☐ in the Dakota apartment building.
   D ☐ on Orchard Street.

4 Thousands of immigrants from Europe came to New York
   A ☐ and found work and a home.
   B ☐ because there was a war in Europe.
   C ☐ and then traveled to other parts of the United States.
   D ☐ but many of them returned to their homeland after a year.

5 In the 1800s the Lower East Side tenements were home to
   A ☐ the Chinese, Italian and Jewish communities.
   B ☐ the Irish community.
   C ☐ immigrants from eastern Europe.
   D ☐ immigrants from Germany.

6 The Ellis Island Immigration Center closed in 1954
   A ☐ and has become a big recreation park.
   B ☐ and has become a museum.
   C ☐ and now the Statue of Liberty stands there.
   D ☐ because immigration to America had stopped.

"For years immigrants had passed through Castle Garden Reception Center"

We form the Past Perfect by using **had** with the **past participle: had passed**. We use the Past Perfect to talk about an action in the past that happened at a time *before* another action in the past.

- *The immigrants **left** Europe after they **had studied** the map of the United States.*

First they studied the map of the USA, and **then** they left Europe.

2 Past Simple and Past Perfect 一般過去時和過去完成時
Use the correct verb tense, either Past Simple or Past Perfect, in the following sentences.

1 Lewis and Clark .... (*spend*) a difficult winter in the mountains because they .... (*lose*) their food supplies.

2 John O'Sullivan .... (*use*) the term "Manifest Destiny" after he .... (*visit*) the West.

3 The pioneers .... (*be*) very tired that night because they .... (*travel*) all day.

4 After a year .... (*pass*) the men .... (*finish*) building the Erie Canal.

5 John Jacob Astor .... (*know*) Manhattan well because he .... (*live*) there for twenty years.

3 Discussion
Discuss the issue of immigration with your class and use these questions to help you.

1 Did people from your country migrate to other lands in the past? If so, where?

2 Is your country receiving immigrants? If so, how is your country helping them? What problems are there?

3 How have immigrants contributed to your country's culture, diversity and work force?

4 What can you do to help immigrants feel at home?

INTERNET PROJECT

Connect to the Internet and go to www.blackcat-cideb.com or www.cideb.it. Insert the title or part of the title of this book into our search engine. Open the page for *American Cities*. Click on the internet project link. Go down the page until you find the title of this book and click on the relevant link for this project.

Divide the class into five groups and each group can research and write a brief report on the following topics on the main menu:

▶ Ellis Island Immigrant Experience
▶ Ellis Island Timeline
▶ Ellis Island Photo Albums
▶ Ellis Island Family Histories
▶ Ellis Island & The Peopling of America

Present your reports to the class and then put them on the class bulletin board. Which group had the most interesting report and why?

Before you read

1 Vocabulary

Match the following words with their descriptions. You can use a dictionary to help you.

1 ☐ boroughs
2 ☐ unique
3 ☐ warehouses

4 ☐ melting pot
5 ☐ residential

A Large buildings where large quantities of goods are kept before selling them.

B Describing a place where there are only homes and no industries or shops.

C Neighborhoods in a big city with their own local government.

D A place where people of different cultures and languages gradually become mixed together.

E Very different, unlike anyone or anything else.

CHAPTER THREE

New York City Today

不眠之紐約

*This is the city that never sleeps
or slows down — it's alive
and bustling with excitement
twenty-four hours a day.*

The City That Never Sleeps

The first thing that a visitor to New York City notices is its international feel with people from all over the world, often in their native dress, who live and work there. You can buy a hamburger from a lady dressed in an Indian sari [1], or catch a cab whose driver comes from Nigeria. Even now in the twenty-first century immigrants and native-born Americans are attracted to this exciting city that never sleeps. The subway is the world's largest, the buses run 24 hours a day and many supermarkets, ice cream shops and restaurants are open 24 hours a day. Something is always happening in the Big Apple [2], day or night.

New York is a city of great differences, where some of the world's richest people live near some of the poorest in the nation.

1. **sari**：莎麗（印度婦女的民族服飾）
2. **Big Apple**：大蘋果（紐約的非正式名稱）

New York City skyline with Brooklyn Bridge on a sunny day.

It is not unusual to see homeless people sleeping in the doorways of skyscrapers. People like actor Robert de Niro and film director Woody Allen call New York City "home". The city is a global centre of international finance, communications, education, fashion, culture and entertainment. Decisions made here usually influence the whole world.

New York City is built on islands and it is divided into five boroughs: Manhattan, Brooklyn, Queens, The Bronx and Staten Island. Each one has individual neighbourhoods, which are unique. The boroughs are connected by tunnels and bridges, like the Brooklyn Bridge or the Verrazano Narrows Bridge.

Manhattan

One and a half million people live on this 34 square mile island (55 km²), where rents are the highest in the nation. It is not difficult to get around Manhattan because most streets run east to west and avenues run north to south.

Lower Manhattan and its busy financial centre, with Wall Street and the New York Stock Exchange, is the oldest part of the city. Ground Zero, where the Twin Towers were before they were destroyed in a terrorist attack in 2001, is in this area.

Chinatown, a crowded, lively neighborhood in the Lower East Side, is the city's largest ethnic community. Like most ethnic communities, Chinatown is like a village in the middle of the big city, where people still know each other by name. The old tenement buildings of the nineteenth century can still be seen in the Lower East Side.

Mott Street runs through Chinatown, where street signs are printed in both English letters and Chinese characters and you can hear people speaking Chinese. Most telephone booths here have roofs like Chinese pagodas. Shops and street stalls sell

Chinatown in Manhattan.

fruit, vegetables and all kinds of Chinese foods and souvenirs. Chinatown is very popular with tourists who love to eat interesting Chinese dishes like Peking duck and chicken with peanuts.

The Chinese New Year's Day Parade takes place each year in late January or early February, according to ancient Chinese tradition, and it is a fantastic event with dancers in original costumes and magnificent fireworks [1].

Manhattan's Little Italy is next to Chinatown, on Mulberry and Grand Streets, with its forty or more Italian restaurants and cafés and old world atmosphere. One of the best times to visit Little Italy is during the last two weeks of September during the Feast of San Gennaro, when the streets are closed to traffic and there is music, dancing, singing and games.

Every Sunday thousands of shoppers go to Orchard Street on the Lower East Side to look for a bargain. Along the sidewalks [2] fashion clothing, shoes and bags are sold at bargain prices. Orchard Street became an outdoor market early in the 1900s when the Lower East Side was a neighbourhood of

1. **fireworks** :

2. **sidewalks** : 人行道

Feast of San Gennaro in Little Italy.

Jewish immigrants who had started the clothing industry in that area. Today the Garment[1] District, where clothes are made and sold, has moved to 7th Avenue (often called "Fashion Avenue") and 34th Street, near Macy's, the world's largest department store. When you walk down "Fashion Avenue" watch out for garment workers who run down the streets pushing racks of clothing[2]! Fashion is a huge business in Manhattan.

Washington Square Park is the heart of Greenwich Village, a colourful neighbourhood with a Bohemian[3] lifestyle. The Village, as New Yorkers call it, has always attracted artists, actors, writers and poets; you can still see the former homes of famous writers like Edith Wharton, Henry James, Mark Twain and Edgar Allen Poe. On weekends crowds of people meet under the Memorial Arch and listen to street musicians, look at outdoor shows or visit art galleries.

Many artists live in nearby Soho, an area of former warehouses. Warehouses make excellent artists' studios because of their high ceilings, big floor space and large windows.

North of Central Park is Harlem, the oldest African-American community in New York with its famous Apollo Theater. During the Harlem Renaissance (1920s-1930s) this neighbourhood attracted important African-American writers, artists and musicians. Although it has been a poor neighbourhood for many years, Harlem is changing and becoming a centre for African-American culture.

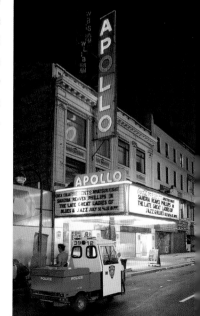

1. **garment** : 衣服
2. **a rack of clothing** :
3. **Bohemian** : 波希米亞

Spanish Harlem or East Harlem, near the Upper East Side, is the city's largest Hispanic community, where people shop in small grocery stores called *bodegas* and read the Spanish newspaper *El Diario*. It is a low-income neighbourhood with many social problems.

Brooklyn, Queens and The Bronx

Brooklyn and Queens are situated on the western tip of Long Island, east of Manhattan.

Brooklyn has been a melting pot for immigrants for almost a century. People from almost every country in the world have created a multicultural borough of about 2.5 million people, who have all, however, become New Yorkers. Queens is a residential area and the home of New York City's two international airports.

The Bronx is north of Manhattan and over half its population is Hispanic. The famous Bronx Zoo, where animals are free to move about, is situated here.

Famous Landmarks

Central Park in the centre of Manhattan is the city's biggest and best-loved park.

The Rockefeller Plaza.

Built in 1876 when most people laughed at the idea of a park in the middle of the city, this beautiful park is where New Yorkers go to relax and get away from the noisy city. Anyone can go to the park and play tennis, baseball or football; to jog, bike, skate, ride a horse, row a boat in the lake, lie on the grass, have a picnic or read a book. Free outdoor concerts and plays are presented here during the spring and summer.

Rockefeller Centre, south of Central Park and situated between 47th and 50th Streets, is a city within a city, with its stores, restaurants and office buildings. During the Christmas season Rockefeller Plaza with its beautiful six-storey-high Christmas tree becomes the city's favourite ice skating rink. The Centre's Radio City Music Hall is the world's biggest indoor theater with 5,900 seats.

World-famous Times Square is where Broadway and Seventh Street cross and it is often brighter at night than at noon because of the big neon signs on the buildings. On New Year's Eve thousands of people meet in the square to celebrate and watch an enormous silver ball drop from one of the buildings at midnight. Times Square with Broadway is the heart of the famous theatre district. There are over thirty important theatres on Broadway that offer musicals and plays, and about twenty "off Broadway" theatres that offer less important and less expensive shows. Tickets for Broadway shows are expensive but theatres often offer half-price tickets on the day of a performance. Every year singers, dancers and actors go to New York with a dream: they want to become stars on Broadway, but only a few are successful.

The magnificent Lincoln Centre for the Performing Arts is situated north of the Theater District in the Upper West Side. Here you can enjoy plays, operas, ballets, modern dance and concerts of all kinds. Madison Square Garden is the world famous stadium that hosts [1] enormous rock concerts, sports events and circuses.

1. **hosts**：主辦

Times Square, which has become a symbol of New York.

New York City Today

Fifth Avenue is probably one of the best known streets in the world; the Empire State Building, once the tallest building on earth and now New York's tallest skyscraper, is situated here. The area of Fifth Avenue, southeast of Central Park, is known as Upper Midtown and contains luxury shops and stores, famous buildings, churches, hotels and museums. Shopping or even window-shopping on Fifth Avenue is an unforgettable experience. The United Nations is situated in Upper Midtown on international ground, with its own postal service and postage stamps.

The Empire State Building, which was completed in 1931.

Time to Eat

You will never be hungry in New York City with its 4,000 or more street sellers, who sell mostly hot dogs and pretzels [1]. The city is famous for its delicatessens [2] where you can buy, among other things, excellent pastrami [3] sandwiches, with New York cheesecake for dessert and an egg cream [4].

1. **pretzels** : 面粉製蝴蝶形酥餅
2. **delicatessens** : 熟食店
3. **pastrami** : 煙牛肉
4. **an egg cream** : 紐約奶昔

35

3 ACTIVITIES

The text and **beyond**

1 Comprehension check

Answer the following questions.

1 Why does New York City have such a cosmopolitan flavor?

2 What do you think the title "The City That Never Sleeps" means?

3 Describe the geographic location of New York City.

4 Describe the neighborhoods located on Mott Street and Mulberry Street.

5 What happens on Sunday on Orchard Street?

6 What is the "Village"?

7 Where can you find the African-American and Hispanic communities?

8 What happens on New Year's Eve in Manhattan?

9 Where can you go to listen to a big rock concert?

10 What can you find on Fifth Avenue?

 **2** Writing

Imagine you are in New York City. This is part of a letter you receive from your best friend.

> Dear...,
>
> How is your vacation in New York City? You're so lucky to be there!
> I have to stay home this summer and work in my parents' shop!
> What's the Big Apple like? What have you seen so far?
> Did you go to Central Park? Have you eaten any special foods?

Write your letter in about 100 words. Answer your friend's questions and include the points below:

- Chinatown and Little Italy
- Greenwich Village and Soho
- Central Park
- your first meal at a delicatessen

T: GRADE 5

3 Speaking: shopping

Fifth Avenue is a wonderful place to shop. Talk about shopping with another student. Ask and answer these questions.

1   What do you like to buy and why?

2   Do you have a favorite shopping area? If so, where is it?

3   How much money do you usually spend in one day?

4   Who do you go shopping with?

4 Listening

Listen to a New Yorker at Central Park talking about his city. Then choose the correct answer — A, B or C.

1   Where is the visitor going after her visit to New York City?

   A   ☐   Arizona

   B   ☐   San Francisco

   C   ☐   Chicago

2   Who made Central Park a safe, clean place?

   A   ☐   the mayor

   B   ☐   the policeman

   C   ☐   the native New Yorker

3   What doesn't the visitor see at Central Park?

   A   ☐   people sitting on the grass

   B   ☐   children playing ball

   C   ☐   signs

4   When is the Jazz Show?

   A   ☐   at half past nine

   B   ☐   at seven o'clock

   C   ☐   at eleven o'clock

5   Where does the visitor come from?

   A   ☐   Chicago

   B   ☐   Arizona

   C   ☐   San Francisco

INTERNET PROJECT

Let's go to the Museum Mile!

The Museum Mile is a lovely area along 5th Avenue from 82nd to 105th Streets on the Upper East Side that has several world famous museums. Let's take a look at some of the more important ones. Connect to the Internet and go to www.blackcat-cideb.com or www.cideb.it. See page 26 for how to find the relevant link.

Divide the class into four groups and each group can research and write a brief report about the current exhibits, collections and any other interesting information about the museum. Present your report to the class and then put it on the class bulletin board. Who had the most interesting report and why?

▶ The Museum of the City of New York
▶ The Metropolitan Museum of Art
▶ The Museum of Modern Art
▶ The Solomon R. Guggenheim Museum

Before you read

1 Vocabulary

Match the following words with their descriptions. Use a dictionary to help you.

1	booming	3	Prohibition	5	alcoholic
2	exposition	4	illegal	6	suburbs

A   Containing alcohol.

B   An international show with industrial products, works of art and other goods.

C   Parts of a city situated outside the center where people live.

D   Growing fast, successful.

E   A period of time in the United States when no one could sell, buy or drink alcoholic drinks.

F   Against the law.

CHAPTER FOUR

Chicago

巨肩之城芝加哥

Its nickname is "the city of the big shoulders" because it's the giant economic and cultural power of the American Midwest.

The Heart of the Midwest

Chicago, Illinois is the largest city in the Midwest, and the third largest in the United States with almost three million people.

    The city, which is the heart of business and industry in the Midwest, was built on the shore of Lake Michigan, America's biggest lake. It is often called the "windy city" because of the strong winds that blow across the city from the lake. The famous American poet Carl Sandburg called Chicago the "City of the Big Shoulders" because Chicago has always done things in a big way: it has the nation's busiest airport, O'Hare; the tallest skyscraper, the Sears Tower; the largest convention centre, McCormick Place, and during the first part of the twentieth century it had the nation's biggest meatpacking industry.

The Sears Tower.

The Beginnings

The name Chicago comes from the American-Indian word Checagou, which means wild onion, a plant which exists in large quantities in the area. Long before the white settlers arrived, the Chicago area was an important transportation area for the Illinois Indians. They traveled in their canoes down the Chicago River to Lake Michigan and along its shores.

Two French explorers, Louis Joliet and Father Jacques Marquette, were probably the first white men to explore the country around Lake Michigan in 1673. The first permanent settler in the Chicago area was an American pioneer, Jean Baptiste Pointe du Sable, who founded the first successful trading post on the north bank of the Chicago River.

In 1803 the United States Army built Fort Dearborn, which became an important trading center that attracted settlers from the East Coast. A village grew around Fort Dearborn and became the town of Chicago in 1833 with a population of 350 people.

Chicago soon became an important railway center between the eastern and western United States with ten major railroad lines, which contributed greatly to its fast growth. The railroads became Chicago's main industry. Products from the industries in New York were easily transported to Chicago by railroad. After the opening of the Galena and Chicago Union Railroad in 1848, products could travel all the way to Iowa in the Midwest. In the 1850s about one hundred trains traveled to and from Chicago daily.

To improve transportation the Illinois and Michigan Canal was built in 1848, which allowed boats from the Great Lakes to travel through the canal and then down the Mississippi River to the Gulf of Mexico. This was an amazing transportation system because it covered about half of the United States.

Open cages and walkways where cattle was kept before being slaughtered in Chicago (1947).

Huge quantities of wheat [1] and corn arrived in Chicago from the Midwest and the city became the nation's major grain market. Live cattle from the Midwest and Texas were sent by railroad to Chicago to be slaughtered [2], and the meatpacking industry became the biggest in the United States. Chicago's booming economy offered jobs to everyone and this brought many new people from rural communities and immigrants from other countries, particularly Germany, Greece, Ireland, Italy and Poland.

At the beginning of the 19th century Chicago did not exist but by the end of the century it was the fifth largest city in the world! Between 1850 and 1890 Chicago's population grew from about 30,000 to over one million.

1. **wheat** : 小麥

2. **slaughtered** : 屠宰

The Great Chicago Fire

During a hot, windy autumn day of October 1871 a huge fire destroyed about a third of the city, including the important business district. Many of the buildings at that time were made of wood and the fire quickly advanced to all parts of the city. One of the few buildings that was not destroyed was the Chicago Water Tower because it was made of limestone [1]; it can still be seen on North Michigan Avenue.

The Great Chicago Fire led to the largest building boom [2] in American history. The people of Chicago started rebuilding their city immediately and in 1885 the world's first steel-frame skyscraper was built, the ten-storey Home Insurance Building. With Elisha Otis's invention of the first safety elevator in 1854 a city could grow vertically, not only horizontally.

In 1893 Chicago hosted the World Columbian Exposition on Lake Michigan to celebrate the 400th anniversary of Columbus's arrival in the New World. The best architects and engineers from all over America went to work at the exposition [3], and many of them remained in Chicago and designed other important buildings. This was the beginning of the famous Chicago School of Architecture. One of these

1. **limestone** : 石灰岩
2. **a boom** : 興盛
3. **exposition** : 博覽會

architects was Frank Lloyd Wright, the father of modern American architecture, who designed unique buildings not only in Chicago but all over the world. The exposition had a great influence on architecture, the arts and the world image of Chicago and America. Only 60 years after its founding, the city was able to host a world fair with almost 200 new buildings.

The Prohibition

The period of American Prohibition started in 1920 and ended in 1933. During the Prohibition it was illegal to produce, transport or sell alcoholic drinks in the United States. But it was not illegal in nearby countries like Canada and Mexico, so some Americans started importing them illegally into the country. Chicago became America's bootlegging [1] centre; dangerous gangsters like Al

---

1. **bootlegging**：非法製造並販賣

The taking of illegal equipment for producing alcohol by Federal agents (1920s).

Capone and his enemy Bugs Moran made millions of dollars. By 1930 Al Capone controlled the huge bootlegging business from Canada to Florida. Murders and shootings were common.

The 1920s, known as the Roaring Twenties, was a period of major industrial growth, prosperity and social change. It was also a time of great musical creativity. The great number of new jobs in Chicago attracted many African-Americans from the southern states.

During the 1960s upper- and middle-class people began leaving the city for the suburbs [1], which was common in many cities across the nation. Some residential neighbourhoods in the centre lost their identity and became slums [2] with serious social problems. Since the 1990s there has been great urban improvement in Chicago's neighbourhoods and many of the slums have been changed into pleasant places to live.

Famous People from Chicago

Chicago has been the home of many famous Americans. Ernest Hemingway, one of the world's great writers and winner of the Nobel and Pulitzer prizes for literature, was born in Oak Park, a Chicago suburb. Other important twentieth-century writers like John Dos Passos and Carl Sandburg were also born in Chicago. Carl Sandburg loved his city and wrote a book of poems about it called *Chicago Poems*. Film producer and director Walt Disney was also a native of Chicago.

1. **suburbs** : 郊區
2. **slums** : 貧民窟

The Magnificent Mile and more

Tourists go to Chicago to admire its architecture; its skyline is among the world's tallest. The Magnificent Mile is situated on North Michigan Avenue between the Chicago River and Lake Shore Drive, and is a mile-long international attraction with architectural landmarks like the Wrigley Building, the Tribune Tower, the 100-storey John Hancock Centre, the Water Tower Place and the Old Water Tower. On the Magnificent Mile there are four shopping centres, museums, fine restaurants and hotels. The Magnificient Mile is the most expensive residential area of Chicago. The Merchandise Mart, the world's largest commercial building and design centre, is nearby. Here you can take a 90-minute guided tour and see the showrooms of America's greatest furniture and gift designers.

View of the Magnificent Mile.

Millennium Park, which opened in July 2004, is a fantastic centre for entertainment, sports, art and music, situated on Lake Michigan. This huge park is a favourite meeting place for the people of Chicago.

Every year in July more than 65 Chicago restaurants open food stalls all over Grant Park so that visitors can try different kinds of food. This fun event is called Taste of Chicago and more than three million people attend it— all tastes are free!

The Chicago "loop", with its large number of skyscrapers, is the downtown area and the second largest business district in America after New York's. The 110-storey Sears Tower, which is in the "loop", is the tallest building in the Western Hemisphere. On clear days you can see parts of other American states from the sky deck; such as Indiana, Wisconsin and Michigan.

You can also get a wonderful view of Chicago from the Hancock Observatory, situated on the 94th floor of the John

The Cloud Gate, a contemporary artwork, by Anish Kapoor in Chicago's Millennium Park.

The famous 'L' train.

Hancock Building. It is the city's only open-air skywalk and it can be very windy up there.

A two-hour boat ride on the Chicago River is one of the best ways to admire the city's unique architecture. If you take the boat on St Patrick's Day on March 17, the river is coloured green in honour of the Irish community.

Another way to see Chicago's downtown is on the "L", the elevated train that was built in 1892 and travels around the "loop" both above the ground and underground.

At the Field Museum of Natural History you can meet "Sue", the world's largest, most complete and best-preserved dinosaur: a Tyrannosaurus rex. The Museum of Science and Industry, the oldest science museum in the Western Hemisphere, is one of the most visited museums in the world.

The Shedd Aquarium, situated on Chicago's Museum Campus, is the world's largest indoor aquarium with more than eight thousand sea animals from all parts of the world.

Don't leave Chicago without trying its most famous dish, Chicago-style deep dish pizza, which was created in the 1940s and is different from any other pizza.

The text and **beyond**

1 Comprehension check

Match the phrases in A with the phrases in B to make complete sentences. There are two phrases in B that you do not need.

A

1. ☐ Carl Sandburg called Chicago the "city with big shoulders"
2. ☐ Fort Dearborn was an important trading center in the early 1800s
3. ☐ In the 1850s Chicago's main industry
4. ☐ Cattle and grain were shipped to Chicago from the Midwest
5. ☐ The Great Chicago Fire caused
6. ☐ The Home Insurance Building was
7. ☐ Frank Lloyd Wright worked in Chicago
8. ☐ The Roaring Twenties and the American Prohibition
9. ☐ Chicago's great architecture can be admired
10. ☐ The world's largest commercial building

B

A   a great building boom in the city.

B   and became the city's leading manufacturing industries.

C   were violent periods with murders and shootings.

D   is the Merchandise Mart.

E   and became one of the world's most famous architects.

F   and was the city's mayor in the 1930s.

G   because it has always done things in a big way.

H   along the Magnificent Mile.

I   is the Museum of Science and industry.

J   and became the town of Chicago.

K   was the railroads.

L   the world's first steel-frame skyscraper.

 **2** The 1920s

Read the text below and choose the correct word for each space. For each question, mark the letter next to the correct word — A, B, C or D.

The Roaring Twenties

The 1920s was a period of social change in America. Although many Americans were (**1**) ...... to old social values of family, home, hard work and the church, a new urban America was growing up in the big cities. F. Scott Fitzgerald (**2**) ...... about these times in his novel *This Side of Paradise* (1920). By contrast, another writer, Sinclair Lewis, wrote *Main Street* (1920), which criticized the boring, small-town life of the American Midwest. Sinclair Lewis was the first American to (**3**) ...... the Nobel Prize for Literature in 1930. The 1920s were a great period for American literature because many writers were inspired by the social changes. Writers like Ernest Hemingway, John Dos Passos, Edith Wharton, Carl Sandburg and William Faulkner became social historians of their times. One of the biggest changes of the twenties (**4**) ...... young women. The new modern woman had short hair, wore colorful clothes, used cosmetics, went to parties and danced to the music of jazz bands. These young women were called "flappers". This (**5**) ...... most parents and older people. This was a time of prosperity and social change. Henry Ford made his famous Model T Ford, the car that everyone could buy. People started to travel more and to (**6**) ...... vacations. More and more people bought their own homes. Newspapers, magazines and the radio improved communications and information (**7**) ...... the nation. Charles Lindbergh's solo flight across the Atlantic Ocean in 1927 was an event that (**8**) ...... a lot of excitement and did much to stimulate the new aviation industry in southern California.

1	**A** tied	**B** held	**C** fastened	**D** united
2	**A** has written	**B** wrote	**C** writed	**D** wroted
3	**A** acquire	**B** achieve	**C** obtain	**D** win
4	**A** considered	**B** noticed	**C** regarded	**D** treated
5	**A** frightened	**B** shocked	**C** jolted	**D** agitated
6	**A** carry	**B** go	**C** bring	**D** take
7	**A** over	**B** between	**C** across	**D** above
8	**A** made	**B** did	**C** caused	**D** resulted

③ Discussion

What were the 1920s like in your country? Use the Internet, a history book or the encyclopedia to help you. Work with a partner and make a list of the important social, cultural, economic and political events that took place during that time. Compare your list with other students.

INTERNET PROJECT

Let's find out more about Frank Lloyd Wright!

Connect to the Internet and go to www.blackcat-cideb.com or www.cideb.it. See page 26 for how to find the relevant link.

Frank Lloyd Wright was one of world's greatest architects; he brought significant changes to the way homes, museums, churches, hotels and buildings were built. Divide the class into eight groups and read Frank Lloyd Wright's biography. Then each group can choose to do a brief report on one of the following buildings: Guggenheim Museum, Imperial Hotel, Johnson Wax Building, Marin Civic Center, Pfeiffer Chapel, Price Tower, Taliesin West, Walker Residence.

At the end of each report write your personal opinion about the building. Which one did you like best and why? Present your report to the class.

The USA: The Birth of Another Music

新音樂誕生地

The United States has the world's largest music industry and millions of people all around the world listen to the music. What has made it so famous? American music is the story of the country, the reflection of a nation alive with growth, change and hope. Its many different styles are the voices of America's multi-ethnic population. In the seventeenth century European immigrants started to bring styles of music and their instruments. Slaves from Africa brought their musical traditions and much of America's modern popular music – blues, gospel, spirituals, jazz, rock – comes from their music.

How and in which cities did the different kinds of music develop?

New Orleans and Dixieland Jazz

The blues is a kind of African-American folk music and a lot of modern American popular music developed from it. The earliest blues was vocal music, without any musical instruments, which the slaves used when they were working on the plantations [1] of the South. Their calls and shouts turned into beautiful but sad songs. Then the blues was mixed with the Christian spiritual songs of African-American churches and this developed into gospel music.

1. **plantations** : 種植園

Early street jazz started in Congo Square in New Orleans in 1835 when slaves met on Sundays to play music and dance. They were allowed to express themselves through music and dance and considered this kind of music to be an expression of freedom.

Brass marching bands [1] were a common tradition in New Orleans long before jazz music started and by 1838 they were on every street corner. These colourful brass bands performed during funerals, Mardi Gras [2], parades and other social events. The bands started using a style known as ragtime [3] and eventually this led to jazz, improvisation and jam sessions [4].

The jazz we know today, was created in the 19th century by the black Creoles [5], who combined the French-Canadian Cajun music with their own styles of music.

1. **brass marching bands**：巡遊銅管樂隊
2. **Mardi Gras**：狂歡節
3. **ragtime**：雷格泰姆音樂
4. **improvisation and jam sessions**：即興演奏
5. **Creoles**：歐非混血兒

Brass Band during Mardi Gras in New Orleans.

Duke Ellington, considered one of the most influential figures in jazz, performs with his orchestra (1943).

Country Music

American country music, sometimes called Western or Cowboy music, is a mix of traditional folk music, Celtic music, blues and gospel; it originated in the Southern United States in the 1920s. Country musicians sang about real-life situations and the songs were often sad. Nashville, Tennessee is considered the capital of country music and hosts a Country Music Festival every year.

Chicago and the Roaring Twenties

Louis "Satchmo" Armstrong started playing jazz with his trumpet on the Mississippi River steamboats and he became extremely popular. In the early 1920s he joined King Oliver, another New Orleans musician, in Chicago, where Dixieland jazz was becoming famous.

During the Roaring Twenties, when America was developing both economically and socially, many African Americans from the southern states moved to Chicago to work. Audiences loved

Louis Armstrong's trumpet, voice and style. He often played for Al Capone in Chicago. Many other musicians tried to copy him, but no one succeeded.

New York and Swing

Jazz began to change in 1935 when white musicians started playing jazz; Benny Goodman played the clarinet [1] with his band in New York. Audiences liked the new sound of the clarinet and the "swing era" was born. Benny Goodman's radio program *Let's Dance* brought the new sound of swing into every American home.

Glenn Miller was a great American musician who created a new sound in music with his clarinet in the late 1930s and early 40s. At this time the United States was experiencing the Great Depression, which brought severe economic difficulties to the nation. The mood [2] of the American people was changing; they were ready for another kind of music. Glenn Miller used the clarinet and several saxophones in his band because he wanted to move away from jazz and create a softer, more melodic [3] sound.

New York City and the Musical

New York City has always been the American capital for musicals and theatre. *The Black Crook* was the first musical performed in New York City, in 1866. There have always been wonderful musicals on

1. **clarinet** : 單簧管
2. **mood** : 心情
3. **melodic** : 旋律

The cast of the musical *Oklahoma!* (1959).

New York's theatre street, Broadway, such as Leonard Bernstein's *West Side Story*, which takes place in Manhattan's Hispanic neighbourhood. Other famous Broadway musicals were *Carousel*, *South Pacific* and *Oklahoma!* by Rodgers and Hammerstein. Many of these musicals became Hollywood films.

1 Comprehension check
Answer these questions.

1 How did the blues start?
2 What happened in Congo Square in 1835?
3 What were the Roaring Twenties like in Chicago?
4 Who created swing?
5 What did Glenn Miller do?

CHAPTER FIVE

San Francisco— The Beginnings

海灣環抱

Surrounded on three sides by water, San Francisco is often called The City by the Bay — the bay that has always played a fundamental role in its history.

In Greek mythology the phoenix was a beautiful bird with red feathers. When it grew old it climbed onto a pile of sticks and set itself on fire. After the fire a beautiful new phoenix appeared. The official seal of San Francisco shows a phoenix because, like the mythological bird, San Francisco has been destroyed several times by earthquakes — in 1868, 1906, 1957 and 1989 — and by many fires. But each time it rises bigger, better and stronger than before thanks to its people.

Yerba Buena

In 1597 the English explorer Sir Francis Drake sailed north of San Francisco into what is now Drake's Bay. He did not see the narrow entrance of San Francisco Bay because of the thick fog that is typical of the area.

View of San Francisco, formerly Yerba Buena, in 1846 before the discovery of gold.

In 1769 Spanish friars [1] founded missions [2] all along the California coast to teach Christianity to the American Indians. During an expedition North, Don Gaspar de Portola and his men discovered San Francisco Bay by chance, one of the largest natural harbours in the world. Seven years later in March 1776 another Spanish explorer, Juan Bautista de Anza, declared that the area of San Francisco was Spain's and built a fort called the *Presidio*.

The Spanish called the new settlement Yerba Buena, because of the sweet-smelling plants that grew there. Soon after, the Spanish friars built Mission San Francisco de Assisi, which today is called Mission Dolores and is the oldest building in the city and the centre of the colourful Hispanic neighbourhood.

Yerba Buena was a small, sleepy village for many years until 1848, when the United States defeated Mexico in a war over land. California became American and Yerba Buena's name was changed to San Francisco.

1. **a friar** : 修士

2. **missions** : 教堂

The Gold Rush

On January 24, 1848, John Marshall discovered gold at Sutter's Mill on the American River about 100 miles (161 km) from San Francisco: this event changed the future of California and the West. Newspaper journalist Sam Brannan brought the exciting news to the sleepy village of San Francisco and on the same day adventurous people with pans and shovels [1] started going to Sutter's Mill to look for gold. In August 1848 a New York newspaper wrote about the discovery of gold in California and the news quickly reached the rest of the nation and the world.

In 1849 thousands of people, later called the "forty-niners" because of the year 1849, invaded the Gold Country hoping to get rich quickly. Some traveled across the Rocky Mountains on horse, covered wagon or even on foot. Many others from all over the world traveled by sea to San Francisco Bay, a journey that took five to eight months. By the autumn of 1849 there were about 600 sailing ships in the harbor and many of them sank. When the Gold Rush began San Francisco had a population of about 900 people; by the end of 1849 the population grew to over 25,000 — and only about 300 were women!

When the adventurous "forty-niners" arrived in San Francisco they immediately went to the Gold Country to look for gold. Most of them did not get rich but a few lucky ones did.

The cleverest people opened banks, eating places, hotels and shops that sold goods to the "forty-niners"; they

1. **a pan and a shovel :**

the miner

farmer, mechanic and cattle raiser all over the west prefer

cut full - honestly made

Levi Strauss & Co's. copper riveted Overalls

the most persistently advertised - the best selling brand. it will pay you to handle the

An advertisement for Levi Strauss & Co's copper-riveted overalls (ca. 1875).

became rich quickly. A German immigrant called Levi Strauss started making strong blue trousers for the "forty-niners"; his trousers were immediately successful and in 1853 he opened his first blue jeans business in San Francisco. Today The Levi Strauss world offices are on the San Francisco Embarcadero.

Saloons [1] and gambling halls opened for the "forty-niners" in a neighbourhood called the Barbary Coast, where Chinatown and North Beach stand today. This was a dangerous neighbourhood known for its crime, outlaws and gambling. During the Gold Rush San Francisco was a wild city and it was difficult to keep law and order.

Keeping law and order was not the only problem. By 1851 there had been six major fires, and then in 1865 and 1868 there were two earthquakes.

Mark Hopkins, Collis Huntington, Charles Crocker and Leland Stanford became San Francisco's richest men during the Gold Rush. They started looking for gold but were not successful, so they decided to open shops that sold goods to the "forty-niners". They soon became very rich and were known as "The Big Four". In 1863 they founded the Central Pacific Railroad, which started building the western part of the transcontinental railroad.

---

1. **a saloon** : 酒吧

Chinese labourers on the Northwest Pacific Railway in the 1880s.

In 1869 the transcontinental railroad was completed and it connected California to the rest of the United States. The railroad contributed greatly to the city's amazing growth and importance. Thousands of men from China who had worked on the railroad settled in San Francisco with their families after 1869 and created the city's Chinatown on Grant Avenue.

Leland Stanford became Governor of the State of California and United States Senator. In 1885 he founded Stanford University, one of the best in the nation.

The 1906 Earthquake

At 5.13 am on April 18, 1906 San Franciscans were thrown out of their beds by a terrible earthquake that measured 8.25 on the Richter scale and lasted about one minute. It killed more than three thousand people and destroyed about 28,000 homes and businesses. The earthquake broke gas lines and fires burned all over the city for several days. Firefighters could do nothing because the water pipes were destroyed. More than half of the city's population of 400,000 were homeless and lived in tent villages for months.

After the terrible earthquake, the famous San Francisco writer Jack London said, "Not in history has a modern imperial city been so completely destroyed. San Francisco is gone."

Earthquakes are common in San Francisco because the city is between the San Andreas and Hayward fault lines; the most recent major earthquake happened on October 17, 1989, which caused 63 deaths and a lot of damage.

View of San Francisco after the earthquake of 1906.

The city was rebuilt quickly after the 1906 earthquake with many improvements in its buildings and structures. By 1915 San Francisco had a new look and hosted the Panama Pacific International Exposition to celebrate the opening of the Panama Canal. The magnificent Palace of Fine Arts, which is a tourist attraction today, was built for the exposition.

Before the Golden Gate Bridge was built, ferry boats were the only way to cross San Francisco Bay. In the early 1900s there was a lot of traffic on the bay because the port was a very busy place and bridges were needed. The Golden Gate Bridge, today the symbol of the city, was called "the bridge that couldn't be built" because of the very strong winds and ocean currents and the possibility of another big earthquake. In 1933 Joseph Strauss, a bridge-builder and engineer, was certain that he could build it. After many difficulties the bridge was completed in May 1937 with a celebration that lasted a week. Strauss was one of the first builders to use safety systems and hard hats for his workers. During the same time another bridge was built, the Bay Bridge that connects San Francisco with the East Bay. These two

Workers during the construction of the Golden Gate Bridge (1935).

new bridges solved most of the traffic problems at that time. Today there are five more bridges that cross San Francisco Bay at different places: the Richmond-San Rafael, the San Mateo-Hayward, the Dumbarton, the Carquinez and the Benicia-Martinez.

A City of Free Thinkers

Through the years San Francisco became the center of America's counterculture [1] which was against conservative government, conformity [2], the social values of the 1950s and the American Dream. In 1953 the poet Lawrence Ferlinghetti opened one of the first independent bookstores in America, City Lights Bookstore in North Beach. There were often lectures and poetry readings, and Monday night was "Blabbermouth Night", when anyone could

1. **counterculture**：反主流文化
2. **conformity**：一致

make a speech. City Lights attracted writers and artists from all over the country. They were tired of middle-class society and called themselves the Beat Generation. They believed that San Francisco promised freedom and excitement. Among them were Jack Kerouac, who wrote *On the Road* in 1957, Allen Ginsberg, Gregory Corso and William Burroughs. City Lights Bookstore is still a meeting place for free thinkers.

The Vesuvio Café is next door to City Lights and is a popular tourist attraction. This is the café where Jack Kerouac and other writers of the Beat Generation used to meet, talk and read poetry. The small road that separates the Vesuvio Café from City Lights has been named Jack Kerouac Alley in honor of the great writer. During the year there are art festivals and shows here.

Bob Donlin, Neal Cassady, Allen Ginsberg, Robert LaVinge, and Lawrence Ferlinghetti (left to right) stand outside Ferlinghetti's City Lights Bookstore in San Francisco.

The text and **beyond**

1 Comprehension check
Answer the following questions.

1 Why does the official seal of San Francisco show a phoenix?
2 Why did the Spanish friars build missions along the California coast?
3 Where was Sutter's Mill and why was it important?
4 What did Sam Brannan do?
5 How did the "forty-niners" reach the Gold Country?
6 Who became rich quickly during the Gold Rush?
7 What was the Barbary Coast?
8 Why are earthquakes common in San Francisco?
9 How was the problem of heavy traffic on the bay solved?
10 What was the Beat Generation?

2 Who did what?
Match the person with the correct description.

A Jack Kerouac
B John Marshall
C Sam Brannan
D Juan Bautista de Anza
E Levi Strauss

F Lawrence Ferlinghetti
G Joseph Strauss
H Sir Francis Drake
I Don Gaspar de Portola
J Jack London

1 ☐ He was an engineer and bridge-builder.
2 ☐ He sailed past San Francisco Bay on a very foggy day.
3 ☐ He discovered gold in 1848.
4 ☐ He accidentally discovered San Francisco Bay.
5 ☐ He built the *Presidio* in 1776.
6 ☐ He was a newspaper editor.
7 ☐ He was a German immigrant who made trousers for the "forty-niners".
8 ☐ He was a famous American writer who saw the San Francisco earthquake.
9 ☐ He was the author of the 1957 novel *On the Road*.
10 ☐ He opened an independent bookstore in North Beach.

PET ③ Routes to California and the Gold Country

Read this text about routes to California and the Gold Country. Decide if each sentence is correct or incorrect. If it is correct, mark A. It if is not correct, mark B.

There were three routes to the Gold Country in the 1850s. A "forty-niner" could go by ship to Panama, cross the dangerous jungle and reach the city of Panama, where he could take a ship to San Francisco.

Another route was much longer. A "forty-niner" could leave New York and make the long sea voyage around Cape Horn, the southern tip of South America, and after seven or eight months reach San Francisco. This was a long, dangerous voyage because of the storms, strong winds and rough sea at Cape Horn. Many small, old ships were used, which often sank. The third and cheapest route was traveling across the continent on the trails that led to California. The greatest number of "forty-niners" walked or rode a horse across the continent. Bad weather conditions and American Indian attacks killed thousands, but by 1852 more than 200,000 "forty-niners" reached the Gold Country. At first there was plenty of gold for everyone — some people made as much as $300 to $400 a day! Some "forty-niners" saved their money in San Francisco banks, but many of them spent it at the Barbary Coast. Life in the mining camps was not easy, and for this reason there were few women and children. The miners often lived in tents or in small wooden houses in poor conditions. Camps like Whiskey Bar, Poker Flat and Rifle Gulch had their own saloon and gambling houses.

		A	B
1	The city of Panama was in the dangerous jungle.	☐	☐
2	The weather at the southern tip of South America was usually bad.	☐	☐
3	People who crossed the American continent spent the least amount of money.	☐	☐
4	Some travelers were killed by the American soldiers.	☐	☐
5	Most of the "forty-niners" who lived in the mining camps were men.	☐	☐

5 ACTIVITIES

PET ④ **Sentence transformation**

For each question complete the second sentence so that it means the same as the first. Use no more than three words. There is an example at the beginning (0).

0   People continued talking about the discovery of gold in California.

People **have not stopped** talking about the discovery of gold in California.

1   Her brother was a good swimmer.
Her brother was .... swimming.

2   No period in American history has attracted so much attention as the Gold Rush.
The Gold Rush has attracted .... than any other period in American history.

3   It was a long train journey to the West.
The train journey to the West .... long time.

4   No one answered his long letter.
He received .... to his long letter.

5   The boy was too young to travel alone on the sailing ship.
The boy was not .... to travel alone on the sailing ship.

INTERNET PROJECT

Panorama of the Destroyed City.

San Francisco's Two Big Earthquakes
Let's take a look at photos of the 1906 and 1989 earthquakes. Connect to the Internet and go to www.blackcat-cideb. com or www.cideb.it. See page 26 for how to find the relevant links.
Go first to the Virtual Museum and working with a partner, click on "16 Views of the Great Earthquake and Fire". Write your impressions.
Then take a look at the photos of the 1989 earthquake on the Geological Survey site. Click on "View photographs on the screen: San Francisco Sites and Bay Bridge". Write your impressions and compare the two earthquakes. What are the similarities and the differences?

CHAPTER SIX

San Francisco Today

今日三藩市

Its geographic position, its colorful history and its open-minded people make San Francisco an exciting place to live.

Today, San Francisco is a dynamic [1], international city with approximately 764,000 inhabitants, one third of them Asian-American. The San Francisco Bay Area, which includes the city of San Francisco and other cities on the coast, is home to over seven million people.

Ever since the days of the Gold Rush, San Francisco has been a friendly, open-minded city. Tourism is the city's biggest business with more than 16 million visitors each year, followed by banking and finance. It is an important cultural and educational centre with many famous museums, concert halls and fine schools. The University of California, Berkeley, is one of the nation's best universities.

San Francisco is unique in many ways. One of its most unusual characteristics is its foggy, windy summers, when temperatures

1. **dynamic** : 充滿活力

don't usually go above 60° F (15 °C) and you can hear the sound of the foghorns [1] that warn ships of dangerous rocks in the bay. The warmest months are September and October, and winters are always mild with no snow or ice. Because of the mild climate San Franciscans can spend a lot of their free time outdoors all year long, exercising, playing sports or just having fun. The good climate means that homeless people have come to San Francisco from all over the nation because they are able to live outdoors.

The City of Ups and Downs

The streets of San Francisco climb up and down 43 hills! Some streets are so steep that steps were built into the sidewalks so that people could walk up and down them. Lombard Street on Russian Hill is very steep and is called the crookedest [2] street in the world; there are a lot of sharp bends. Visitors love driving down this one-way street.

View of Lombard Street.

In 1873 Andrew Hallidie, an engineer, created a special transportation system, the cable car, which is one of the city's biggest tourist attractions. He designed cable cars that are moved by an underground cable and travel at 9 miles (14 km) per hour, uphill and downhill. Most of the cable cars in

1. **foghorns** : 霧笛
2. **crookedest** : 最彎曲

People standing on the running boards of the cable cars.

use today were built in the nineteenth century and have seats for only about 30 people. Many more passengers enjoy standing on the outside running board, holding on to the poles. The cable car bell is a sound much-loved by San Franciscans. The cable car is the only moving National Historic Landmark in the USA. San Francisco has a fast modern subway system called BART (Bay Area Rapid Transit System), with lines that go under the bay and connect the cities of the Bay Area.

The Embarcadero

Since San Francisco is at the tip of a peninsula [1] water is never far away. The ocean and the bay are too cold and full of sharks for most swimmers, but sailing and wind-surfing are popular sports thanks to the strong west winds. Most of the city's unique attractions are on the Embarcadero, the beautiful walkway on the long waterfront. The name Embarcadero comes from the Spanish verb *embarcar* which means get onto a ship or put things onto a ship.

Fisherman's Wharf [2] is another very popular area on the bay with fishing boats, restaurants, seafood stalls, shops and street

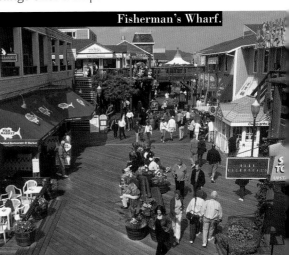

Fisherman's Wharf.

1. **a peninsula** : 半島
2. **a wharf** : 碼頭

performers. Sea lions [1] are often seen swimming near the fishing boats and they welcome any food from visitors.

Pier 39 was an old wooden pier [2] that was transformed into the main attraction at Fisherman's Wharf. Its 110 specialty shops, 12 restaurants and wonderful ice cream shop were built on two levels. The famous Christmas Store on level one sells Christmas trees of all colors and of all sizes all year long.

You can get a fantastic view of the Golden Gate Bridge, Bay Bridge and Alcatraz Island and smell the salty sea air from Pier 39. You can also visit the amazing Aquarium [3] of the Bay and walk through its long acrylic [4] tunnels under the bay and see more than 20,000 marine animals, including sharks, as they swim in their natural habitat.

At the Wharf there are ferry boats that take you to Alcatraz Island, which opened in 1934 as a maximum security prison for America's most dangerous criminals. No prisoners ever successfully escaped from Alcatraz because of the icy waters of

1. **a sea lion** : 海獅

2. **a pier** : 碼頭

3. **an aquarium** : 水族館

4. **acrylic** : 亞克力樹脂

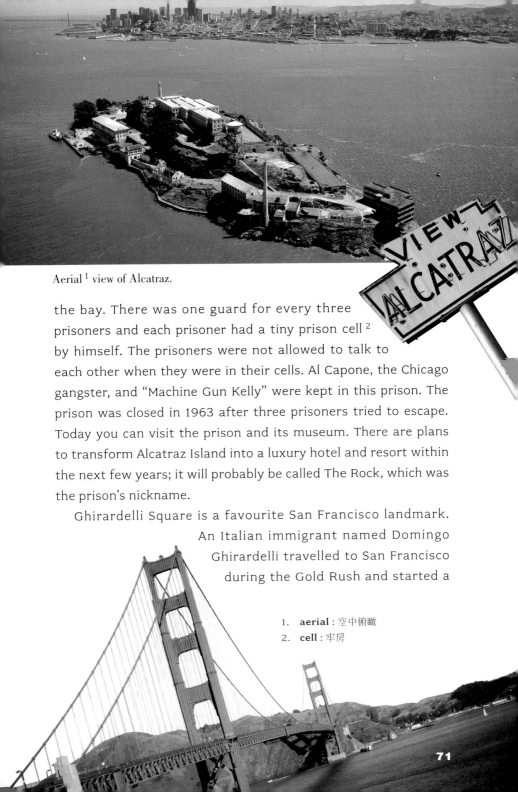

Aerial[1] view of Alcatraz.

the bay. There was one guard for every three prisoners and each prisoner had a tiny prison cell[2] by himself. The prisoners were not allowed to talk to each other when they were in their cells. Al Capone, the Chicago gangster, and "Machine Gun Kelly" were kept in this prison. The prison was closed in 1963 after three prisoners tried to escape. Today you can visit the prison and its museum. There are plans to transform Alcatraz Island into a luxury hotel and resort within the next few years; it will probably be called The Rock, which was the prison's nickname.

Ghirardelli Square is a favourite San Francisco landmark. An Italian immigrant named Domingo Ghirardelli travelled to San Francisco during the Gold Rush and started a

1. **aerial** : 空中俯瞰
2. **cell** : 牢房

chocolate business, which grew quickly. In 1889 his sons bought a whole block of land near the bay and built their redbrick chocolate factory. Today, Ghirardelli Square is famous for its chocolate and ice cream, in addition to its fine art galleries, shops and restaurants.

North Beach, Chinatown and Downtown

North Beach, which is not a beach at all, is the city's Italian neighborhood, filled with Italian sidewalk cafés, food shops and restaurants. Columbus Avenue starts at Fisherman's Wharf and continues through North Beach, passing Washington Square, which is a lovely park and meeting place for the people of the neighborhood. North Beach is the city's liveliest neighborhood and was home to the artists and writers of the Beat Generation. There is still a Bohemian flavor and an open-minded attitude here.

Telegraph Hill, which is the heart of North Beach, was an important signal station during the Gold Rush that told people of the arrival of ships with mail, goods and passengers. Today Coit Tower, built in honor of San Francisco's firefighters, stands on top of the beautiful hill near some of the city's most expensive homes.

Coit Tower and Telegraph Hill.

A dragon
in the Chinese
New Year
parade.

Chinatown is next to North Beach, where Grant Avenue meets Columbus Avenue. It is the oldest Chinese neighbourhood in the United States and also one of the biggest outside the Orient. Chinatown is noisy and colourful all year long with street lights that look like lanterns [1] and street signs also written in Chinese characters. Most buildings and houses have Chinese-style roofs and the narrow streets are crowded with people, shops, restaurants and vegetable and fruit stands — there is always a smell of good food in the air.

Chinese New Year is celebrated with a huge parade in January or February, like in New York.

Walking south on Grant Avenue or Stockton Street you will see Union Square, one of the most famous shopping areas in the world with its expensive shops. At Christmas time there is an enormous Christmas tree in the middle of the big square. Union Square's name goes back to the time of the American Civil War (1861-1865), when San Franciscans who supported the Union Army met here.

1. lanterns : 燈籠

Market Street, another perfect place for shoppers, is only one block away.

Montgomery Street is sometimes called the Wall Street of the West. It is the heart of San Francisco's financial district. The city's tallest skyscraper, the 52-storey Bank of America building, is located here, near the unusual Transamerica Pyramid. This pyramid-shaped skyscraper is home to offices and shops and has become another symbol of the city.

The Haight

The Haight-Ashbury neighborhood is famous for its historic Victorian houses called "the painted ladies" and its liberal attitude. During the late 1960s young people who called themselves hippies or "flower children" came to live here: they dreamed of a world full of peace and love. During the so-called "Summer of Love" in 1967 more than 100,000 young people from all over the world went to the Haight for a huge open-air party that continued for weeks. Famous rock groups like Jefferson Airplane and the Grateful Dead were formed in the Haight at that time.

Famous view of the Victorian "Painted Ladies" from Alamo Square.

The text and beyond

PET ❶ **Comprehension check**
For each question choose the correct answer — A, B, C or D.

1   What is San Francisco's oldest form of transport?

    A ☐ the underground train

    B ☐ the cable car

    C ☐ the BART

    D ☐ the car

2   Until 1963 Alcatraz Island was a

    A ☐ museum.

    B ☐ signal station.

    C ☐ luxury hotel.

    D ☐ jail.

3   Which neighborhood attracted artists and writers?

    A ☐ North Beach

    B ☐ Chinatown

    C ☐ The Embarcadero

    D ☐ Union Square

4   Where was the 1850s signal station located?

    A ☐ Washington Square

    B ☐ Telegraph Hill

    C ☐ Grant Avenue

    D ☐ Ghirardelli Square

5   When did Union Square get its name?

    A ☐ during the Gold Rush

    B ☐ during the 1906 earthquake and fire

    C ☐ in 1874

    D ☐ during the American Civil War

6   The "Summer of Love" was

    A ☐ a party outside.

    B ☐ in the early 1960s.

    C ☐ organized for American hippies.

    D ☐ a one-day music concert.

6 ACTIVITIES

2 Listening
Listen to Carol, a San Franciscan tour guide, tell visitors some
important facts about the City by the Bay. Then decide if the
sentences below are true (T) or false (F). Correct the false ones.

		T	F
1	There are seven islands in the San Francisco Bay City limits.	☐	☐
2	Visitors are not allowed on the Farallones.	☐	☐
3	Angel Island is a marine sanctuary for all forms of sea life.	☐	☐
4	The city's first lighthouse was Alcatraz Island.	☐	☐
5	The Bay Bridge crosses Yerba Buena Island.	☐	☐
6	The Bay Bridge was not damaged during the big 1989 earthquake.	☐	☐
7	San Franciscans are very worried about earthquakes.	☐	☐
8	The Golden Gate Bridge is visible in the fog.	☐	☐
9	Café Trieste is a favorite meeting place for celebrities.	☐	☐

INTERNET PROJECT

Have fun in San Francisco!
Connect to the Internet and go to www.blackcat-cideb.com or
www.cideb.it. See page 26 for how to find the relevant link.
Divide the class into two groups and explore two great places in the
city: Golden Gate Park and the Cable Car Museum.
The first group can go to Golden Gate Park, the city's biggest park, and
research the Conservatory of Flowers, the de Young Museum of Art, the
Japanese Tea Garden in Golden Gate Park and write a brief report.
The second group can click on Cable Car Heritage and find out about
cable cars and the famous bell ringing contest. Write a brief report and
enjoy the pictures.
Then present your reports to the class. Which place would you prefer to
visit and why?

The Rock and Roll Revolution

搖滾起義

Elvis Presley (1956).

"Rock 'n' Roll" developed in the United States in the late 1940s and early 1950s, and included various kinds of popular music: gospel, blues, folk, jazz and country. It influenced not only music but lifestyles, fashion, language and attitudes.

The recording by Bill Haley and His Comets of "Rock Around the Clock" in 1955 started the Rock 'n' Roll revolution. The song became one of the most successful in history and a huge number of teenagers went to see the performances.

In January 1956 Elvis Presley's first single record, "Heartbreak Hotel" was released and by April of that year one million copies were sold in the United States. Teenagers loved Presley's voice, his clothes and the way he moved when he sang; the girls liked his good looks.

Newspapers described his performances as "vulgar [1]" and many parents were afraid he was a bad influence on young people.

Presley sang hundreds of rock 'n' roll songs during his career and also made several Hollywood films. Although there have been many rock 'n' roll singers, he is still "The King of Rock 'n' Roll".

1. **vulgar** : 低俗

The 1960s, '70s and beyond

In the 1960s British bands such as The Beatles, The Who, The Rolling Stones and Led Zeppelin became very popular and had a big effect on American culture and music. The music industry was changing and most songs were not written by professional composers any more but by singers. Popular music was considered an art and not just a form of business and entertainment.

Musical movements of this period and their singers, like Pete Seeger and Bob Dylan, were connected to politics such as civil rights and the opposition to the Vietnam War. Many of these musical movements were part of the counterculture, the opposition of what was considered "acceptable" in society, and connected to the hippies and flower children. In San Francisco

Bob Dylan.

the Grateful Dead and Jefferson Airplane were two counterculture musical groups that were formed in the Haight-Ashbury neighbourhood.

In the 1970s rock singer and songwriter Bruce Springsteen from New Jersey became a famous star with his songs that are about the social problems of the poor and the working class.

Metallica and Megadeth, America's first heavy metal bands, were formed in Los Angeles and San Francisco in the early 1980s, and today this type of music is still very popular.

Hip-hop music, also known as rap, began in the Bronx, in New York City in the 1970s among African Americans and Latino Americans. It is a very rhythmic kind of music and uses a voice that speaks rhythmically and in rhyme.

New music styles and groups are formed all the time in the United States as a result of a very active entertainment business; some become very popular while others disappear after a short time.

1 Comprehension check
Answer these questions.

1 Why was Rock 'n' Roll considered a revolution?
2 Why did Elvis Presley become so popular?
3 Which British bands influenced American music?
4 Who were the singers and groups connected to the politics of the 1960s and '70s?
5 What are Bruce Springsteen's songs about?
6 Why are many new music styles and groups born in the United States?

Before you read

PET

1 Listening

Listen to the first part of Chapter Seven and choose the correct answer A, B or C.

1 How has Los Angeles grown?

A ☐ vertically

B ☐ horizontally

C ☐ in both directions

2 How do people get around in Los Angeles?

A ☐ by car

B ☐ by bus

C ☐ on the subway

3 What do Los Angeles and San Francisco have in common?

A ☐ warm climate

B ☐ earthquakes

C ☐ many hills

4 Who lived in the Los Angeles area before the Spanish explorers arrived?

A ☐ Friar Junipero Serra

B ☐ the Chumash American Indian people

C ☐ the Mexicans

5 What attracted settlers to Los Angeles in the late 1870s?

A ☐ the movie industry

B ☐ jobs on the Southern Pacific Railroad

C ☐ the warm climate and fertile land

6 Where did orange trees grow?

A ☐ in the San Fernando and San Gabriel valleys

B ☐ in the Wilmington Fields

C ☐ in Whittier Narrows

CHAPTER SEVEN

Los Angeles

天使之城

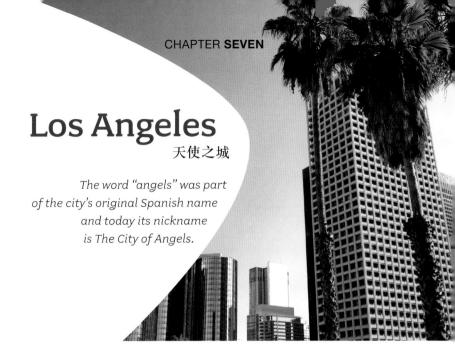

*The word "angels" was part
of the city's original Spanish name
and today its nickname
is The City of Angels.*

Los Angeles, often called L.A., is the largest city in California with almost 3,900,000 people and the second largest in the United States after New York City.

It is a great multiethnic centre with a very large Hispanic population. Los Angeles County, which includes 88 other well-known cities, is the biggest in America with about 12 million people. The port of Los Angeles is the busiest in the United States.

The city covers an amazingly large area: 44 miles (71 km) north and south, and 29 miles (47 km) east and west; it is an excellent example of a city that has grown horizontally more than vertically. Due to the city's size Angelenos[1] move around by car and traffic is always heavy, creating a lot of smog. Since it rains very little and there is almost no wind, the smog increases

1. **Angelenos** : 洛杉磯人

Smog over the city of Los Angeles.

in the air, making Los Angeles the most polluted city in America. Many Angelenos work in Los Angeles but live in the suburbs [1] and have a long commute [2] every day — sometimes as long as three or more hours.

Los Angeles, like San Francisco, is built on several earthquake fault lines, the San Andreas Fault and others, which cause about 10,000 earthquakes every year. Fortunately Angelenos do not feel most of them because they are very small. The most recent major earthquakes were the Whittier Narrows earthquake of 1987 and the Northridge earthquake in 1994.

The Beginnings

The Chumash American-Indian people lived in the Los Angeles area when the Spanish explorers arrived in the late 1770s. In 1771 Friar Junipero Serra built the Mission San Gabriel Arcangel

1. **suburbs** : 郊區
2. **commute** : 往返上下班

in the San Gabriel Valley, and in 1781 the Spanish governor Felipe de Neve founded "El Pueblo de Nuestra Senora la Reina de los Angeles de Porciuncula" (The Town of Our Lady the Queen of the Angels on the Porciuncula River) nearby. The small Spanish town became a rich farming and cattle area. After the Mexican-American War in 1848 Los Angeles and California became part of the United States.

In the 1870s Los Angeles was still a village of about 5,000 people who worked on farms or cattle ranches. The arrival of the Southern Pacific Railroad in 1876 contributed greatly to L.A.'s growth. Several new railroad lines connected southern California with the rest of the United States and settlers from the East Coast and the Midwest travelled to Los Angeles, attracted by the sunny warm climate all year long and a lot of rich land. In the spring of 1886 one railroad line charged only one dollar to travel from Kansas City to Los Angeles! The westward growth to southern California was very fast — from 1880 to 1900 the population grew from about 11,000 to over 102,000. New cities

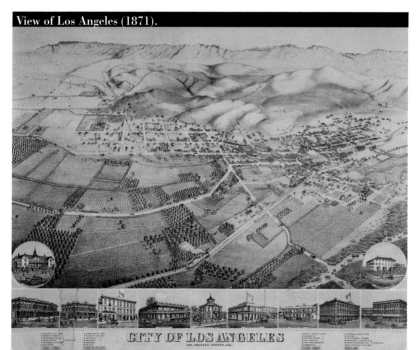

View of Los Angeles (1871).

CITY OF LOS ANGELES

developed around Los Angeles: Pasadena, Santa Monica, Pomona, Redondo Beach and Long Beach.

In the 1900s inexpensive commuter[1] trains connected the new cities with the suburban areas; automobiles, roads and freeways later replaced the trains.

The discovery of oil in Los Angeles by Edward L. Doheny in 1892 started the booming oil industry, which brought great wealth to the city. Today there are still several active oil fields like the Wilmington Oil Field, which is the fourth largest in America. With plenty of cheap oil the automobile and rubber industries grew quickly and there were more jobs for more people.

During the same period a unique agricultural economy developed. Orange trees and other fruit were grown on thousands of acres[2] of land in the San Fernando and San Gabriel valleys. These products then traveled by train to the East Coast where there were big markets for them.

1. **commuter** : 往返上下班的乘客
2. **acres** : 英畝

California oil wells near Los Angeles (1910).

The Motion [1] Picture and Aircraft [2] Industries

The first motion picture theatre in California opened in Los Angeles in April 1902. In the early 1920s Los Angeles became well known for two of America's most important 20th-century industries: motion pictures and aircraft.

Motion picture producers moved their studios from the East Coast to Los Angeles to take advantage of the excellent weather and beautiful filming locations — palm trees, exotic [3] flowers, ocean beaches, deserts, snowy mountains. Hollywood, on the western edge of the City of Los Angeles, and Culver City, farther south and closer to the ocean, became the centres for movie production.

By the end of the 1920s seven important studios — Metro-Goldwyn-Mayer, 20th Century Fox, Warner Brothers, Paramount, Columbia, Universal and RKO — had created

1. **motion** : 動
2. **aircraft** :
3. **exotic** : 外來

Movie set in Hollywood (1922).

the biggest motion picture industry in the world. This was the "golden age" of Hollywood, where each studio employed thousands of actors, actresses, writers, musicians, camera operators and costume designers. By the 1930s the exciting motion picture industry was simply called "Hollywood" and it produced over 400 films a year. The movie industry was the start of the huge entertainment business which later included television as well.

Howard Hughes, one of America's richest men and best pilots, founded the Hughes Aircraft Company in 1932 in Culver City in West Los Angeles. It became one of America's biggest aircraft industries, and during and after World War II it employed a great number of people in Los Angeles County. In 1948 Hughes founded the Aerospace Group, which built aircraft for travel, defense and space exploration. Hughes was also an important Hollywood film producer and director of films like *Scarface* and *The Outlaw*.

L. A. Today

When people think of Los Angeles the first thing that comes to mind is Hollywood and its movie stars and rock idols. The best place to see more than 2,000 five-pointed stars is the Hollywood Walk of Fame, a sidewalk along Hollywood Boulevard and Vine Street. Inside each pink star on the sidewalk is the name of a celebrity — usually an actor, actress, singer or dancer but the cartoon character Mickey Mouse has a star too!

Grauman's Chinese Theater, which looks like a red Chinese pagoda, is Hollywood's most famous movie theater with almost 200 handprints, footprints[1] and autographs[2] of Hollywood stars in the cement[3] in front of the theater. Visitors like looking for their favorite star's handprint or footprint and touching it.

Another famous Los Angeles theater is the beautiful Kodak Theater, built in 2001. It is situated on Hollywood Boulevard. This 3,332-seat theater hosts the important Academy Awards event, when the best actors,

1. **handprints, footprints**：手印，腳印
2. **autographs**：簽名
3. **cement**：水泥

A residential area in Beverly Hills.

actresses, directors and costume designers receive the Oscar. Each year more than 40 million Americans watch the event on television.

But visitors who expect Hollywood to be an exciting city filled with movie stars and rock idols are disappointed because it is not exciting at all. Hollywood should not be confused with Beverly Hills, which is a few minutes drive away. This is where the stars live, in beautiful mansions on famous tree-lined streets like Roxbury Drive, Bedford Drive and Benedict Canyon Drive. They usually shop on Rodeo Drive, the world's most famous and expensive shopping area. Some of the shops here ask customers to make reservations before they come to shop. Beverly Hills is a beautiful neighbourhood for the very rich and famous: Paris Hilton, Tom Cruise, Christina Aguilera, Britney Spears and "Sly" Stallone to mention a few. There are no ugly buildings, industries, billboards [1], or even hospitals in Beverly Hills.

1. **billboards**：戶外廣告板

The celebrities who do not own a home in Beverly Hills usually own one in Malibu Beach, a 21-mile band of coastline on the Pacific Ocean. Their magnificent homes are on the beautiful beach in front of the Pacific Ocean, with a guarded gate at the entrance to keep people out; the name on the gate says "Malibu Colony". Leonardo DiCaprio, Bruce Willis, Steven Spielberg, Whoopi Goldberg and Mel Gibson are just a few of the residents. Most of these homes are usually second homes or vacation beach houses.

The Third Street Promenade is a pedestrian street in Santa Monica that has become a huge shopping mall with hundreds of fine shops. People from all over Los Angeles County go there to shop and to enjoy the tall palm[1] trees, the flowers, the long beach and the ocean. When you're tired of shopping you can enjoy lunch or dinner in one of the many eating places, or watch street performers.

The Los Angeles coast line is famous for its free beaches and beach towns like Manhattan Beach, Santa Monica, Redondo Beach and Venice Beach, which are perfect for surfers.

---

1. **palm**：棕櫚

A surfer on Venice Beach.

The text and **beyond**

1 Comprehension check
Answer the following questions.

1 How many cities make up Los Angeles County?
2 How does smog form and why is it a problem?
3 How did the railroad contribute to the development of the Los Angeles area?
4 What is the oil industry like in Los Angeles today?
5 Why are the San Gabriel and San Fernando valleys famous?
6 When and where did the motion picture industry begin and how did it develop?
7 What is the Hollywood Walk of Fame?
8 How are Hollywood and Beverly Hills different?
9 What is Rodeo Drive like?
10 What is the "Malibu Colony"?

2 Vocabulary
Complete the definitions (1-10) with a word from the text.

1 Another word for petroleum: _ _ _
2 People who live in Los Angeles: _ _ _ _ _ _ _ _ _
3 Polluted air: _ _ _ _
4 Another word for films: _ _ _ _ _ _
5 A citrus fruit: _ _ _ _ _ _
6 A long journey to go to work: _ _ _ _ _ _ _
7 A city where movies are made: _ _ _ _ _ _ _ _ _
8 The signature of a famous person: _ _ _ _ _ _ _ _ _
9 A famous shopping area: _ _ _ _ _   _ _ _ _ _
10 Marks made by your feet: _ _ _ _ _ _ _ _ _ _

PET 3 Notices

Look at the text in each question. What does it say? Mark the correct letter — A, B or C.

1

Academy Awards
tonight at 8 pm
No admittance
after 7:45 pm
(Black Tie Event)

A ☐ The show starts at 7.45 pm for men with black ties.

B ☐ If you arrive after 7.45 you cannot enter.

C ☐ The show will start earlier than usual.

2

RICH REWARD!
$50,000
for lost pink poodle.
If found please call:
392-0369

A ☐ If you call 392-0369 you will receive $50,000.

B ☐ If you lost a pink poodle call 392-0369.

C ☐ You will receive money if you find the pink poodle.

3

Los Angeles
Safari Park
No Feeding
Animals In Forest

A ☐ You are not allowed to give food to the animals.

B ☐ Animals are not allowed in the forest.

C ☐ Animals must not eat in the forest.

4

MALIBU BEACH
COLONY
Trespassers will be
fined and detained.

A ☐ To you enter the colony you must pay.

B ☐ If you enter the colony a guard will arrest you.

C ☐ If you enter the colony a guard will stop you.

5

RODEO DRIVE SHOES
We only receive clients
with appointments made
a fortnight in advance.
Call mornings only except
for Saturday.

A ☐ You can buy shoes in the morning only.

B ☐ You must make an appointment 15 days ahead of your visit.

C ☐ The shop is not open on Saturday.

T: GRADE 5

4 Speaking: entertainment

Los Angeles County is the world capital of entertainment — movies, television, music, recording studios, theaters. Work with a partner and present a short report to the class about the role entertainment plays in your life. Use the following questions to help you.

1   What is your favorite kind of entertainment?

2   Why do you like it?

3   How much money do you spend on this kind of entertainment?

4   What is the entertainment capital of your country?

5   How is it different from Los Angeles?

INTERNET PROJECT

Let's visit the Theme and Water Parks in Los Angeles!

There are four major theme parks and four water parks in the Los Angeles area that are unique attractions.

Connect to the Internet and go to www.blackcat-cideb.com or www.cideb.it. See page 26 for how to find the relevant link.

Divide the class into eight groups and each one can do a brief report on a theme park or water park: Disneyland, Knott's Berry Farm, Universal Studios, Six Flags Magic Mountain, Knott's Soak City, Wild Rivers Waterpark, Raging Waters and Hurricane Harbor. Present your report to the class. Which theme or water park was most fun? Put your reports on the class bulletin boards.

American Cities in Films

電影中的美國城市

Ever since Hollywood started making films almost a century ago the world has been watching American movies. The American film industry is the largest in the world and huge amounts of money are spent on film making. Some of the greatest films in movie history have been filmed in American cities that provided the perfect setting for the story. In fact, the city is often the protagonist along with the actors and actresses.

San Francisco

The City by the Bay, with its steep hills, foggy weather, tall bridges and unforgettable skyline has inspired many movie directors. Alfred Hitchcock's masterpiece *Vertigo* (1958), a thriller about an almost-perfect murder, was filmed in San Francisco. One of the most dramatic scenes takes place at the foot of the Golden Gate Bridge when Kim Novak jumps into the icy waters of the bay and is saved by James Stewart. Another thriller by Alfred Hitchcock is *The Birds* (1963). It was filmed at Bodega Bay, a tiny, foggy town on the Pacific Ocean near San Francisco.

In the police thriller *Bullitt* (1968), starring Steve McQueen, San Francisco's steep hills are the scene

James Stewart and Kim Novak in the rescue scene in *Vertigo* (1958).

93

Scene from *The Rock* (1996).

of an extraordinary car chase down Lombard, Leavenworth, Filbert and Mason Streets. Another police thriller filmed in San Francisco's North Beach, Russian Hill and Twin Peaks is *Dirty Harry* (1971), starring Clint Eastwood.

Many movies have been filmed on Alcatraz Island. *Escape from Alcatraz* (1979), starring Clint Eastwood and Patrick McGoohan, was inspired by the true story of the escape attempt by prisoners Frank Morris and John and Clarence Anglin on June 11, 1962. The FBI believed they drowned although no bodies were ever found. After this escape attempt Alcatraz Penitentiary was closed.

The *Birdman of Alcatraz* (1962), starring Burt Lancaster, was also filmed on Alcatraz. It was inspired by the true story of Robert Stroud, who kept canaries [1] in his cell and wrote two books about them while he was a prisoner at Alcatraz.

Another action movie featuring a wild car chase on San Francisco's steep hills and an incredible adventure on Alcatraz Island is *The Rock* (1996), starring Sean Connery and Nicholas Cage.

Pacific Heights (1990) was a thriller starring Melanie Griffith and Michael Keaton, about a psychopath [2] who rents an apartment in a beautiful house in the exclusive Pacific Heights neighborhood in San Francisco.

1. **a canary**：金絲雀

2. **a psychopath**：精神病患者

New York City

New York City has been the protagonist of a great number of films of all kinds. One of the greatest movies is *The Godfather* trilogy, directed by Francis Ford Coppola and based on Mario Puzo's novel about southern Italian immigrant families who settled in Little Italy and became involved in the Mafia, the criminal organization also known as Cosa Nostra in the United States.

One of America's greatest film directors, Martin Scorsese, has set many of his films in New York: *Mean Streets* (1973), *Taxi Driver* (1976), *New York, New York* (1977), *Raging Bull* (1980), *The Age of Innocence* (1993) and *Gangs of New York* (2002). His films represent New York City during various historical periods, but the central themes are always violence—physical and psychological—corruption, gang wars between immigrants and problems caused by ethnic differences.

Woody Allen, another famous movie director, was born in New York City and loves it dearly. He has made some of his best movies there. *Manhattan* (1979) is a tribute to his city and some critics have said that New York City is the main character of the film.

New York City's impressive skyline and tall skyscrapers have been the perfect setting for blockbuster films like *King Kong* (2005), *Spiderman* (2002) and *Independence Day* (1996), to name only a few.

Woody Allen and Diane Keaton in a scene from *Manhattan* (1979).

Robert de Niro as Al Capone in *The Untouchables* (1987).

Chicago

Many films set in Chicago involve the Mob [1] during the Roaring Twenties. Some are comedies like *Some Like It Hot* (1959), directed by Billy Wilder, which the American Film Institute listed as "the greatest American comedy of all times". The Oscar-winning musical *Chicago* (2002), starring Catherine Zeta-Jones, Renée Zellweger and Richard Gere, was set in that city during the Roaring Twenties. Other films are much more violent and serious, like *The Untouchables* (1987), about a brave Federal Agent who wants to arrest Al Capone during the Prohibition era.

An exciting manhunt [2] movie starring Harrison Ford is *The Fugitive* (1993), which is filmed in downtown Chicago with great views of the "loop", the Magnificent Mile, the "L", the Sears Tower and the Chicago River colored green on St Patrick's Day.

Los Angeles and Hollywood

Los Angeles is the world capital of the movie industry and has been the favorite setting for thousands of films. In the 1920s, when the movie industry was just starting, many films were set in Los Angeles and the surrounding area.

For many years the streets of Los Angeles have been the setting for classic private detective films, such as *The Big Sleep* (1946), with detective Philip Marlowe. Another excellent private detective film with a complex plot is *Chinatown* (1974), directed by Roman

---

1. **mob** : 有組織犯罪
2. **manhunt** : 追捕

Polanski and starring Jack Nicholson.

Films like *The Player* (1992), starring Tim Robbins and *LA Confidential* (1997), starring Russell Crowe, are "movie movies"— they are films that are about Hollywood, the movie business, its actors and inside secrets. In *The Player* more than 60 actors, actresses, directors and producers appear in the film for a few minutes and say a few words.

The hot, smoggy weather and the crowded freeways of Los Angeles are the setting for *Falling Down* (1993), starring Michael Douglas, the story of an ordinary man caught in heavy commuter traffic who starts going mad.

All the glamour of Beverly Hills and the luxury of Rodeo Drive are beautifully shown in *Pretty Woman* (1990), starring Julia Roberts and Richard Gere, parts of which were filmed at the Beverly Wilshire Hotel on Wilshire Boulevard.

1 Comprehension check

Look at the chart below. It has been divided into seven major film categories. List the films that were mentioned in the dossier according to their genre. You may not be able to list all of them.

Police Films	
Thrillers	
True stories about people	
Organized Crime	
Private Detectives	
Comedies	
Musicals	

CHAPTER EIGHT

New Orleans

悠閒的新奧爾良

*Mark Twain once said,
"An American has not seen
the United States until
he has seen Mardi-Gras
in New Orleans."*

New Orleans, the largest city in Louisiana, is one of America's most unique cities because of its unusual geographic location. Lake Pontchartrain lies north of the city and the Mississippi River lies south; half of the city is below sea level and some scientists say it is slowly sinking! New Orleans is often called "The Big Easy" because of its relaxed way of life. Its population today is about 240,000, which is fifty percent less than before hurricane Katrina. New Orleans is one of the largest and busiest ports in the world. There are oil rigs [1] nearby in the Gulf of Mexico and there are several important oil refineries near the city. However, tourism is the city's biggest business.

New Orleans has a humid, subtropical climate with short mild winters and hot, humid summers; and October is the driest month.

1. **an oil rig**：石油鑽機

The Beginnings

La Nouvelle-Orléans was the French name for New Orleans, which was founded in 1718 by the French Mississippi Company on the east bank of the Mississippi River and south of Lake Pontchartrain; it was named after Philippe II,

New Orleans in 1949.

Duke of Orléans. In 1763 New Orleans became part of the Spanish Empire and most of the unique architecture that can be seen today in the French quarter is from the Spanish period. After the Louisiana Purchase of 1803 New Orleans became part of the United States. Its economy, like that of the other states of the South, was based on sugar and cotton grown on big plantations [1]. The sugar and cotton were then taken to the port of New Orleans, put on ships and steamboats and sold in other parts of the United States and the world. Some of these old plantations with their beautiful mansions are historical landmarks and can be visited today.

In the 1800s New Orleans was a major trading port because of its position on the Mississippi River. Steamboats and barges [2] constantly travelled up and down the Mississippi River transporting goods to and from New Orleans.

During the War of 1812, the British understood the importance of New Orleans's position on the Gulf of Mexico. They sent an army to take command of the city but during the big Battle of New Orleans in January 1815 the American army won.

1. **plantations** : 種植園
2. **barges** : 駁船

Before the American Civil War (1861-1865) New Orleans was the largest slave [1] market in the country and slave traders [2] became rich very quickly. In 1860 there were more than 330,000 black slaves in the state of Louisiana; most of them worked on the plantations.

The location of New Orleans near the Gulf of Mexico coast makes it vulnerable [3] to hurricanes and other tropical storms. In 1718 the city started to be built on high ground on the east bank of the Mississippi, but as the population grew the city moved into the area of Lake Pontchartrain, a huge swamp [4] area below sea level. Homes in New Orleans do not have cellars or basements because there is always water right under the house.

Keeping Water Out

In the early 1900s engineers studied the geographic problems of New Orleans. They knew that if the city had good pumps and strong levees and floodwalls [1], it would be safe for its

1. **slave** : 奴隷
2. **slave traders** : 奴隷商販
3. **vulnerable** : 易受攻擊
4. **swamp** : 沼澤

Greater New Orleans Louisiana suspension bridge across the Mississippi River.

inhabitants. They started building pumps to get rid of the extra water. They built about 350 miles (560 km) of levees and floodwalls to keep water out of the city half of which is below sea level. Unfortunately, these pumps, levees and floodwalls did not work against the force of hurricane Katrina in 2005, which flooded and destroyed 80% of the city and killed 1,464 people.

After this natural catastrophe the American government started building better pumps and stronger floodwalls. Many private individuals who love New Orleans gave money to help rebuild the city. Actor Brad Pitt started the "Make It Right" project with his own money to redevelop parts of city and give homes to families who lost theirs. He plans to build one hundred and fifty new inexpensive homes in the Ninth Ward, a part of the city that was destroyed by the hurricane. Former United States President Bill Clinton is working with Brad Pitt on this project. Brad Pitt has been a frequent visitor to New Orleans in the past and likes the city and its people very much. He and his partner Angelina Jolie own a mansion in the French Quarter of the city, which was not destroyed by Katrina since it is situated on higher ground.

The French Quarter

The French Quarter with its narrow streets is also known as the Vieux Carré ("old square" in French); it is the site of the original settlement. It is a National Historic Landmark and was hardly touched by hurricane Katrina because of its location. Lovely houses of different colours with cast-iron balconies [2] and exotic

---

1. **levees and floodwalls** : 堤壩和防洪牆

2. **a cast-iron balcony** : 鑄鐵陽臺

plants, trees and flowers show French, Spanish and Creole [1] architecture. The French Quarter's central plaza is Jackson Square, with its statue of Andrew Jackson, an American hero of the War of 1812, and St Louis Cathedral, built in 1794.

Visitors love walking down Canal, Royal, Bourbon, Chartres and Decatur Streets with their shops, art galleries, museums, bars, live music, exciting night life, friendly people and Creole restaurants [2]. The French Quarter is famous for its music, ragtime and jazz, which were born here at the beginning of the 20th century. The French open-air market, with its European flavor, was set up in 1791 and is the oldest public market in the United States; here you can buy fruit, vegetables, souvenirs and clothing. At the western end of the French Quarter is Canal Street, which divides the Quarter from the city's business district.

La Place du Marché Francais

French Market Place.

1. **Creole**：法、西、非、印第安文化的混合風格
2. **Creole restaurants**：混合風格餐廳

Bourbon Street
in the French Quarter
of New Orleans.

One of the best ways to get to know America's longest river, the Mississippi, and see the skyline of New Orleans is to ride the *Natchez*, a 19th-century steamboat that travels along the river. One of the best ways to see the Audubon Park and Zoo, and the Garden District with its beautiful 19th-century mansions and gardens, is to take the St Charles Streetcar, which has been traveling on St Charles Avenue for over 165 years.

National Protected Areas

Bayou Sauvage National Wildlife Refuge is a 23,000-acre area situated within the city of New Orleans. It is the largest urban wildlife center in the United States, and it is only fifteen minutes from the French Quarter. Hundreds of different kinds of birds, fish, alligators, reptiles and amphibians live in these protected swamps all year long. Every year almost half a million tourists from all over the world visit this protected area.

Jean Lafitte National Historical Park and Preserve protects the rich natural and cultural resources of Louisiana's Mississippi River area, which is divided into six separate areas.

Cypress trees in Bayou Sauvage National Wildlife Refuge area.

The New Orleans Jazz National Historical Park is located near the French Quarter and shows visitors the origins and history of jazz. At Perseverance Hall No. 4 visitors can see where black jazz musicians and their bands played music for black and white audiences many years ago.

Mardi Gras

America's great writer Mark Twain once said, "... an American has not seen the United States until he has seen Mardi Gras in New Orleans."

Mardi Gras in New Orleans is one of the most famous carnival celebrations in the world and attracts over a million visitors every year. The date of Mardi Gras changes from year to year, but always falls between February 3 and March 9. Mardi Gras, the French term for "Fat Tuesday", started in the 1700s as a Christian festivity and today it has its own flag and colors: purple, green and gold. The city is beautifully decorated for the event and everyone takes part in the fun. Although Mardi Gras is a particular day, the term includes a much longer period of celebrations that lead up to that day. The Carnival season includes amazing parades, beautiful costumes, live music, masked balls, dancing and fun in the streets. On the day of Mardi Gras the famous Rex Parade walks through the crowded streets and is followed by several other fantastic parades.

Viewers fill balconies in the French Quarter for Mardi Gras.

The text and **beyond**

1 Comprehension check

Match the phrases in A and the phrases in B to make complete sentences. There are two phrases in B that you do not need.

A

1 ☐ The city of New Orleans is located

2 ☐ Its position on the Mississippi River near the Gulf of Mexico

3 ☐ New Orleans became part of the United States

4 ☐ In the 1800s New Orleans was

5 ☐ The old part of the city

6 ☐ Homes in New Orleans do not have cellars

7 ☐ Pumps, levees and floodwalls were built in the 1900s

8 ☐ Hurricane Katrina

9 ☐ The largest urban wildlife center in America

10 ☐ Mardi Gras is the name of a specific day

B

A   was built on high ground on the east bank of the Mississippi River.

B   but carnival celebrations go on for many days before.

C   because there is always water under them.

D   makes it vulnerable to hurricanes and tropical storms.

E   after the Louisiana Purchase of 1803.

F   destroyed a good part of the city and killed many people.

G   is in the French Quarter.

H   belonged to the Spanish government.

I   to keep water out of the city.

J   between a lake and a river.

K   is only fifteen minutes from the French Quarter.

L   a busy port and a huge slave market.

2 Louis Armstrong

Read about Louis Armstrong's youth and how his career started. Then fill in the gaps with the words in the box.

> apartment audiences fame group instruments jobs
> joined nickname noticed raised success talent trouble

Louis Armstrong, the Famous Son of New Orleans

Louis Armstrong, whose (1) .... was "Satchmo" or "Pops", was born in New Orleans on August 4, 1901, to a very poor family.

His father left the family when Armstrong was born and he was (2) .... by his mother and grandmother in the slums of New Orleans. He left school after the fifth grade and worked at different low-paying (3) .... As a young boy he liked music and listening to bands. He joined a (4) .... of boys who liked singing and they sang in the streets for money. When he was twelve he got into (5) .... and was put in an institute for young boys with discipline problems. Here he was given a small trumpet to play in the institute's band. He quickly learned to play it very well and learned other musical (6) .... too.

In 1917 his musical talent was (7) .... by "King Oliver", a trumpet player who played a kind of music known as New Orleans Jazz or Dixieland Jazz. Soon Armstrong met other musicians like "Kid" Ory and Bunk Johnson, and he started playing on the riverboats of the Mississippi River. He joined the Fate Marable Band, which was well known at that time, and his musical (8) .... grew. By the time he was twenty he had learned to read music and had started playing trumpet solos. He was one of the first jazzmen to do this and he created a new, unique sound that (9) .... loved. Soon he started singing and playing and his performances were always a (10) .... In 1922 Armstrong (11) .... King Oliver and his Creole Jazz Band in Chicago and made his first recordings with Oliver the next year. Chicago was a prosperous city in the 1920s and Oliver's band was the best hot jazz band; people ran to listen to Armstrong and his success grew. For the first time in his life he had his own (12) .... with his own private bath. No one could play the trumpet like Armstrong and he was on his way to international (13) ....

"If the city had good pumps and strong floodwalls, it would be safe for its inhabitants."

When we think about a situation in the present or future which is unreal, unlikely or hypothetical we use the second conditional:
If + past tense of the verb, *would* + verb
Look at these examples:

- **If** there **were** fewer cars in the French Quarter, there **would be** less traffic and smog.
- **If** I **knew** the phone number of the hotel on Jackson Square, I **would book** a room.

3 Write a sentence with *if* for each situation. The first is done for you.

1 We don't visit Lafitte Historical Park very often because it is far away.

If Lafitte Historical Park wasn't far away, we would visit it more often.

2 It's raining hard so we can't take the steamboat ride on the Mississippi River. ....

3 Susan doesn't work at the New Orleans Tourist Office because she doesn't speak French. ....

4 The city has problems because it is built below sea level. ....

5 Mark wants to take part in the Mardi Gras Parade but he doesn't have a costume. ....

T: GRADE 5

4 Speaking: music
New Orleans is well known for its music. Work with a partner and talk about music. Use the questions below to help you.

1 What kind of music do you listen to?

2 Do you play a musical instrument or do you sing?

3 Do you have a friend who plays an instrument or sings?

4 Who is your favorite performer — musician or singer?

5 How many hours a day do you spend listening to music?

6 How often do you go to concerts — rock or classic?

1 **Fact File**

What facts do you remember about the five American cities you have read about? Look at the files and fill in the gaps; some facts are already there.

---

1 | **Population**

New York: 8, 275,000. It is the [1]............... city in the United States.

Los Angeles City: [2]............... .

Los Angeles County: [3]............... . It is the [4]............... county in the United States.

Chicago: 3,000,000. It is the [5]............... city in the Midwest.

San Francisco: 764,000

New Orleans: [6]............... About [7]............... of the population left after hurricane Katrina.

---

2 | **Geography**

New York City was built on islands and is divided into [8]...............
boroughs: [9]............... .

Los Angeles's extension is amazing: [10]............... miles east and west and [11]............... miles north and south.

Chicago is built on America's largest freshwater lake, [12]............... .

San Francisco is a [13]..............., surrounded on three sides by water.

New Orleans is located between a lake, [14]..............., and a river,
[15]............... .

---

3 | **Geographic problems**

San Francisco is located between two [16]..............., the [17]...............
Fault and the [18]............... Fault.

Los Angeles is located on several [19]............... .

About half of New Orleans is [20]............... sea level.

---

4 | **Nicknames** (you can write more then one)

Los Angeles: City of Angels and [21]............... .

New York: [22]............... .

San Francisco: [23]............... . (but don't call it 'Frisco!')

Chicago: The Windy City and [24]............... .

New Orleans: [25]............... .

5 | **First Settlers**

New York: [26] ....   Los Angeles: [27] ....

Chicago: [28] ....   New Orleans: [29] ....

San Francisco: [30] ....

6 | **Important Sites** (list as many as you can)

New York: Greenwich Village, [31] ....

Chicago: Merchandise Mart, [32] ....

San Francisco: Pier 39, [33] ....

Los Angeles: Beverly Hills. [34] ....

New Orleans: [35] ....

7 | **Famous Shopping Areas** (list as many as you can)

New York: [36] ....   Los Angeles: [37] ....

Chicago: [38] ....   New Orleans: [39] ....

San Francisco: [40] ....

8 | **Famous People Associated with the City**

New York: [41] ....   Los Angeles: [42] ....

Chicago: [43] ....   New Orleans: [44] ....

San Francisco: [45] ....

2 **Identify the picture**

Look at these pictures and identify them with the city or a specific site.

1   New York
2   Chicago
3   New Orleans
4   San Francisco
5   Los Angeles

3 **What do you think?**

What in your opinion is unique about the five cites you have read about? Discuss it in the class.

4 **Discussion**

What is the geography of your city or town like? Is it built on hills, like San Francisco; on a huge, windy lake like Chicago; or is part of it below sea level, like New Orleans? Work with a partner and write some geographic facts about your city or town. How has its geography influenced its development and growth? What is unique about your city or town? Compare your work with other students.

5 Crossword puzzle.

Across

2 strong transparent plastic

4 famous beach where celebrities live

7 boat with a flat bottom

8 live well and make money

10 another word for clothing

12 San Francisco's old name

13 big celebration in New Orleans

15 big luxurious home

16 America's biggest lake

Down

1 at high risk

3 long trip to go to work

5 system of transportation

6 someone who is careful with money and spends it wisely

7 making and selling illegally

9 very wet land with plants and trees

11 land where Indians went to live

14 bird from Greek mythology

17 movies are made here

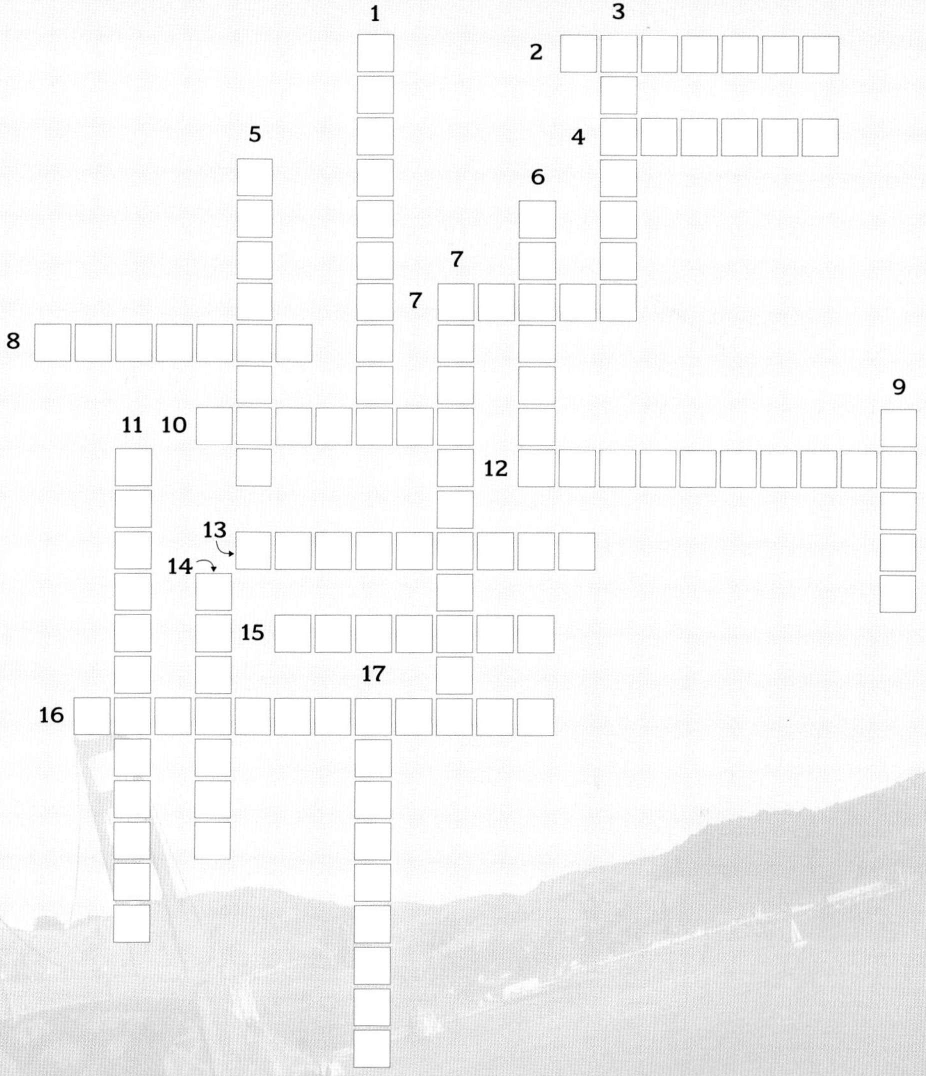

Answers to quiz — page 15

1 C 2 B 3 C 4 A 5 B 6 C

Black Cat Discovery 閱讀系列：

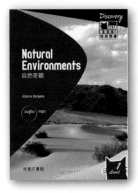

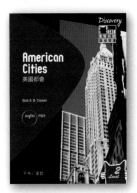

Level 1 and 2